The Sharp Empire IV

Return of the Gospel

Tyler Johns

Order this book online at www.trafford.com
or email orders@trafford.com

Most Trafford titles are also available at major online book retailers.

Printed in the United States of America.

ISBN: 978-1-4907-2491-1 (sc)
ISBN: 978-1-4907-2490-4 (e)

Trafford rev. 01/14/2014

www.trafford.com

North America & international
toll-free: 1 888 232 4444 (USA & Canada)
fax: 812 355 4082

CHAPTERS

PROLOGUE

PRAISE FOR THE SHARP EMPIRE

Emperor Hieronymus Sharp, half-cobra half-lizard, came to be and ran this evil empire with his evil sorcery. His soldiers, pirate knights, were sent to steal a dead body that was revived inside a robot. The robot with the body was known as Darth Waternoose. Together, Emperor Sharp along with his followers won many wars against those that defied his power. The emperor wanted to eliminate children's fantasies and destroy many worlds created for them.

One day, a team of freedom fighters working for the Heaven Federation, stood up to the Sharp Empire. A lioness named, Nala Boomer, an orangutan with the title, Skinamarinky-Dinky-Dink Skinamarinky-Doo, and a large wasp named, Zinger Warsp, were sent to investigate.

On the Death Scale, the Sharp Empire's biosphere and ultimate weapon, Boomer met an alien dragon named,

Dermazzo Joustiáño, who became her master in training to fight the Serpential forces. But Joustiáño betrayed Boomer and joined the empire as a count. Boomer was executed by a machine called the Spruce Noose, in which she was hanged. Skinamar and Zinger escaped the Death Scale and returned home to the Heaven Federation.

A few years later, the Sharp Empire once again reigned over the Milky Way. War was planned against a royal family in Ireland. After the fall of the king and queen, their children, Martino and Mariana Izodorro went their separate ways. Betrayed by some of her people, Princess Mariana was kidnapped by the Serpential forces. Prince Martino stayed with his aunt and uncle on their farm.

The Heaven Federation needed a new team of freedom fighters. As Princess Mariana was rescued to work with the Federation, she and a band of spies were assigned to steal plans that were made for the Death Scale. The princess was captured once again.

Skinamarinky-Dinky-Dink Skinamarinky-Doo and the freedom fighters' robot, the Invisi-Bot, went to Earth and landed in Ireland, where they found the princess's elder brother, Martino Izodorro. Zinger Warsp appeared with them and gave them gifts for fighting against the Sharp Empire. And so, they all left into space and formed a new team; joining them were Captain Tiblo Tigro (a tiger), Shana Cargon (a kangaroo with intelligence), and Manda Monka, an alien wolf whose family was murdered (on their home planet fourth of the Sirius system). The last to join them was a European medical scientist, a human named Regulto Beauxon, who is cursed to transform into a beast by taking his invented medicine of courage.

The freedom fighters attempted to rescue the princess from the Serpentials, but they were too late. The Serpentials executed the princess by letting her drown in Lake Prisoner. Robots used a freezing substance to trap the princess in a prism of ice. She was up and floating to the air like a satellite. The white condor god, Artidector, planned to bring the princess back to life. The freedom fighters were given powers and individual fighter ships to fight against the Serpential forces.

They rejoined the Heaven Federation in their base on a horse head nebula within Orion. The Death Scale approached as both sides fought each other in war. The battle ended as Martino destroyed the Death Scale according to the assignment. The Death Scale was broken into four major pieces. Victory went to the Heaven Federation.

A year later, the Federation had a base underwater on a newborn cold planet. The Sharp Empire planned an attack with a fleet of submarines. The Federation escaped. The freedom fighters were assigned to recover artifacts known as gem scales that were to hold the Death Scale together. They recovered two and placed them in their rightful places.

Meeting with the Serpentials, the freedom fighters met Count Joustiáño, who challenged them in a fight and won against them. In this situation Manda Monka's front paws were chopped off by Joustiáño's light saber. She had them replaced with bionic paws in a hospital ship.

Later, the freedom fighters were assigned to recover the last gem scale, which belonged in the bio-dome of the nasty place filled with dead guts called, Gutville. After that, the Death Scale was in the process of coming back together.

In the meantime, a new enemy arrived to meet the freedom fighters. He was known as Brain Tentacles, a mutant alien mixed with a giant brain for a head with a beard of tentacles. There was a horde of mixed aliens; they included Manda's father, Genghis Monka, revived with parts of different aliens. He warned the freedom fighters about the aliens after a mysterious gem held in a canister. That gem contained the Phantom of the Galaxy. Artidector revived Nala Boomer for her new destiny and another hero for the freedom fighter team, Steve Irwin, the Australian crocodile hunter who once died from the sharp tail of a bull ray.

After recovering the galactic ghost gem, the freedom fighters met up with Tiblo's old school friend, Pangera Pelwoski the panther, who was ordered to lure them into a trap planned by the Sharp Empire. The freedom fighters were taken hostage as Tiblo was placed in a chamber in which he was frozen in a crystal and taken by Count Joustiáño and the shell-lacking turtle bounty hunter, Carpoon.

After Artidector's training with them, Boomer and Irwin went to where the freedom fighters were taken hostage. Irwin joined the freedom fighters as Boomer faced Darth Waternoose for a duel. Pangera joined the team and led the others out of the city of Heloid as Darth

Waternoose won the duel with Boomer, leaving her a cut from his light saber across her belly. Boomer rejoined the freedom fighters and was fixed up in a hospital ship. The freedom fighter team was increased.

Tiblo Tigro, frozen in a crystal was taken to the planet Treetop and into a palace owned by a henchmonster named, King Owpi. Joustiáño and Carpoon had him guard the galactic ghost gem.

Now is the time for the final battle . . .

CHAPTER 1

REBUILDING THE DEATH SCALE

The freedom fighters of the Heaven Federation fly to the planet, Treetop, farthest from the Death Scale, in order to rescue Captain Tiblo Tigro from the clutches of the pig-like henchmonster, King Owpi Caudalosaurus. Little do the freedom fighters know is that the Sharp Empire had planned a modification for an even more powerful biosphere than the first Death Scale. Now that it is complete, the freedom fighters might struggle to restore freedom to the Milky Way . . .

The Death Scale was put together once again by recovery of the gem scales. A shuttle arrived into one of the docking bays of Serpentopolis as Serpential officers waited. The shuttle had Darth Waternoose riding in it. Governor

Kalvino Kassow confronted the shuttle and stood as Waternoose walked out after landing.

"My lord," said the governor, "our biosphere is together again for more destruction."

"We will dispend the Heaven Federation with our ultimate power," said Waternoose.

"We will hire specialists," said the governor. "Eventually our victory will be announced."

"The emperor will be here for that," said Waternoose. They walked forward together and contacted a senator by a computer. The screen turned on.

"Senator Vacklepuss here," said a cassowary senator talking in the screen.

"Prepare our biosphere with our greatest power," said the governor.

"We shall do our best," said the senator. The screen turned off.

And so, in outer space rejoined in the Great Red Shark on their way to planet Treetop, farthest from the Death Scale, the freedom fighters of the Heaven Federation were working. Shana Cargon helped with an upgrade on the Invisi-Bot.

"That should do it, Vizzy," she said putting on the robot's metal covering. "All fixed."

The Invisi-Bot pressed a button that tested his untouchable force field that penetrated his body.

"Excellent! Marvelous!" he said. "Now I can get back to work."

Skinamar was at a computer scanning for locations, by looking at the three planets that followed the Death Scale.

He listened to rock music on a nearby radio. Martino along with Pangera Pelwoski, was at the cockpit.

"Young man," said Pangera, "ain't that music getting on your nerves? I have to concentrate on finding Tiblo."

Martino smiled and looked at Pangera saying, "Okay, old cat." He turned back and said, "Turn it down, Skinamar!"

Skinamar turned the radio's volume low. Suddenly, he picked something up on the scanner.

"Hey!" he shouted. "I think I found something!" Everybody went to him and looked at the computer.

"That must be King Owpi's palace," said Martino.

"Well, what are we waiting for?" said Pangera.

"We must find Tiblo," said Manda.

"Captain Tigro must still be frozen in that crystal," said the Invisi-Bot.

CHAPTER 2

KING OWPI'S PALACE

And so, the Great Red Shark was landed on the planet Treetop. Skinamar and the Invisi-Bot were the first two to go ahead and follow the path that led to the palace of King Owpi.

"Why are we the first to move ahead?" asked the Invisi-Bot.

"Because Marty said that you're the machine and I'm the jester holding the message," said Skinamar.

"That explains a lot," said the Invisi-Bot. "My joints are cracking."

Suddenly, they found the palace. It was mostly made up of green wood with domes of mud bricks. Skinamar and the Invisi-Bot stood in front of the entrance gate.

"Are you sure this is the right place, Skinamar?" asked the Invisi-Bot.

"Positive," said Skinamar.

The Invisi-Bot knocked on the gate. A hatch opened next to it and a security camera popped out. The Invisi-Bot went to it.

"Identify yourself," said the camera.

"Um uh . . . I am called the Invisi-Bot and I have an orangutan," he answered.

"Very well," the camera replied. "Proceed." It went back in its socket. The gate suddenly hovered up slowly for our heroes' entry.

"Finally," said Skinamar as he hopped inside.

"Skinamar, wait!" said the Invisi-Bot as he waited for his size of the gate's height to open and ran in.

And so, they were both in. They got confronted by two guards that looked like hog-nosed orcs. They crossed their axes guarding the heroes' path.

"King Owpi will be pleased to see you," said one of the guards. "Follow us." Skinamar and the Invisi-Bot followed the guards to Owpi's throne room. There were reptiles, amphibians, and therapsidian beasts sitting around. Owpi with the face of a pig, a scaly body, four arms and a large tail supporting his weight, was surprised to see visitors.

"Welcome," he said. "Make yourselves comfortable . . . if you have something for me."

"As a matter of fact, we do, sire," said Skinamar. He took out a message plate, which came from the other freedom fighters. "A message from my friend, Marty." He played the message:

"Greetings, mighty King Owpi, I am Martino Izodorro, a freedom fighter of the Heaven Federation. I am recording this on behalf of my missing friend, Captain Tiblo Tigro. I also bring you a special gift, this robot and orangutan . . ."

"What??" said the Invisi-Bot with a reaction.

". . . You are a great and powerful ruler, Owpi. My father was once."

"Skinamar, you're playing the wrong message," said the Invisi-Bot.

"This is the only one I saw him record," Skinamar replied. The Invisi-Bot grabbed the message plate and turned the knob back and forth to see some certain problems. It was all about Martino talking.

"Oh, whatever!" the Invisi-Bot scolded as he stopped and turned it off.

"Well, that's our message," said Skinamar.

"Make yourselves useful," said Owpi. "Boys! Our guests need some entertainment."

A band of tough beasts, mostly reptiles, arrived to set up band instruments. They were about to sing a song. A keyboard was being played along with a deep-toned horn. A caiman was the first to sing one verse:

"Yo! The name is Glash, I battle with a
lash I am a very clever caiman
I come up and say, 'Hey, Man!"

This is a rap song. The next verse was sung by a big fat crocodile:

"Hello, this is Magnus, I came to nag
us. Got a shiny bald mace

This is such a great place."

A blue frog with black spots sang next:

"They call me Dart Wart, I'm a poison dart frog."

The last was a cynodont (reptile with fur from prehistoric Earth):

"I'm Pelosaur, a lizard with fur I growl
like cur and we're all in a bog."

Together the beasts sang the chorus:

"We're the Swamp Thugs . . . Huh, huh huh.
We're the swamp thugs of planet Treetop."
Magnus: *"Get a load of our swamp*
grass we catch some fishy bass."
Dart Wart: *<Croak>* *<Croak>*
Glash: *"Yeah! Yeah! We're slopping . . ."*
Together: *"We're the Swamp Thugs."*

The music met the end and faded out.

"Whoa!" said Skinamar. "What a rap."

"Also, sire," said the Invisi-Bot to King Owpi, "we would like to see our captain, Tiblo Tigro."

"Ah!" said Owpi. "See for yourself. He's in a temporary condition . . . decorating my palace."

Skinamar and the Invisi-Bot witnessed Tiblo still frozen in the giant crystal.

"Look, Skinamar," said the Invisi-Bot. "Captain Tigro. And he's still frozen in that crystal."

"Take them to the dungeon!" Owpi commanded his guards and they did.

Chapter 3

Prisoners

As the guards showed Skinamar and the Invisi-Bot to a dungeon cell, the two found different rooms with torture. A tortoise was having his shell scraped.

"No! No!" he cried. A rolling blade chipped one scale of his shell and the tortoise screamed.

The guards placed Skinamar in one cell as a robot approached them and spoke to the Invisi-Bot.

"Are you suitable in calculations and technology?" the robot asked.

"Uh . . . yes," the Invisi-Bot answered.

"How many languages do you speak?" the robot asked.

"Uh . . . about 2,000 to be precise," said the Invisi-Bot.

"This robot will be in need of the king."

The guards headed for the exit of the dungeon.

"Skinamar, don't leave me!" the Invisi-Bot cried as he was being carried out.

"I'll get us outta here," said Skinamar. ". . . somehow."

A moment later, a group of mysterious bounty hunters arrived in the palace. Regulto Beauxon and Steve Irwin were held in wrist binders.

"We are here to take prisoners for you," said the purple-robed bounty hunter.

"Oh dear!" said the Invisi-Bot horrified at the bounty hunters holding Regulto and Steve.

"Very well," said Owpi. "They'll fit nicely with the orangutan."

The bounty hunters took Regulto and Steve to the dungeon. They put them in the cell with Skinamar.

"Guys!" said Skinamar in surprise.

"Skinamar!" said Regulto.

"I'm glad to see you," said Skinamar.

"Blimey!" said Steve smelling the dungeon cell. "Who keeps dead matter around here?"

"Just some weird reptiles," said Skinamar.

"How are we going to get out of here?" asked Regulto.

"I'll think of a plan," said Skinamar, "if I knew our friends were gonna be here."

The black-suited bounty hunter looked through his mask for the expected company. The brown-suited hunter hopped next to him. The purple-suited hunter looked at the crystal with Tiblo frozen inside it.

"We must wait until nightfall when Owpi and his guards fall asleep," said the black-suited hunter.

"Then our captain will rejoin us, right?" said the brown-suited hunter wagging her tail. The hunters waited until the night came.

Chapter 4

Freeing Tiblo

Owpi and his hand men were all asleep. The purple-suited bounty hunter came to the crystal with Tiblo. She found the button pad next to a channel grid on the base box that held the crystal on top of it. She typed in a certain code that would turn the machine off and melt the crystal. After typing the code, the bounty hunter stepped away as the crystal started melting. The machine was deactivated. Tiblo turned red and the crystal melted faster. Tiblo was burned in some areas of his body and clothing. His fur was singed as well. He jumped off the box and landed on the dirt of the palace's floor.

"Aah," said Tiblo as he felt burned. The bounty hunter went to him and lifted him onto her lap.

"Just relax," she said. "You are free from the crystal chamber."

"Ow, what's going on here?" Tiblo spoke out.

"My partners and I are protecting you from a monster," said the bounty hunter.

"Where am I?"

"The palace of King Owpi, our thirtieth henchmonster."

"Who are you?"

The bounty hunter took off her mask. It was Manda. She was in disguise the whole time.

"One of your best scouts," she said.

"Manda," said Tiblo.

Suddenly, evil laughs filled the room. Owpi and his henchmen found the two animals reunited.

"So," said Owpi, "a reunion of two heroes, eh?"

"You must be King Owpi," said Tiblo. "I heard all about you."

"Indeed," said Owpi.

"I'm here to take my captain back," said Manda. The minions kept laughing.

"My scouts might need me," said Tiblo.

"Patience, you'll be with them eventually," said Owpi. "Take him to the dungeon!" The guards took Tiblo to the dungeon as commanded.

"As for you, pretty one," Owpi turned at Manda, "you'll be rather comfortable sitting in my lounge. Tuck her away!" He commanded his guards and they did. In the lounge, they tied her paws and gagged her as they placed her on a couch. As the guards took Tiblo to the dungeon, he was placed in the same cell with Skinamar and Regulto. He suddenly witnessed them.

"Skinamar?" he asked. "Regulto??"

"Captain!" Skinamar and Regulto both said in surprise.

"You guys!" said Tiblo as he skidded closer to them. "Am I glad to see you?"

Meanwhile, a hooded figure entered the palace, walking toward King Owpi. The figure removed his hood. It was Martino.

"King Owpi," he said.

"Ah, you must be the one called, Martino Izodorro," said Owpi.

"Indeed I am," said Martino.

"What can I offer you?" asked Owpi.

"My friends in pursuit of releasing Captain Tiblo Tigro."

Owpi laughed. "You wouldn't dare bother me about that, would you?"

"You will bring Captain Tigro and the others to me, or be destroyed. It's your choice."

"Your offer cannot be made." Owpi pressed a button on the arm of his throne. It opened a trapdoor under Martino. He fell through it along with one of the guards. They both slid on a slide down into a sewer below the palace. They were in green water. Something huge and scary was creeping toward them. A gigantic, mantis-like monster with long fangs emerged by stepping each long leg into the water by splashing it with four feet one by one. It had a loud deafening screech.

CHAPTER 5

A DARING ESCAPE

The horrendous monster lunged toward Martino and the guard. The guard screeched out and hissed with his forked tongue to cry for help, but the sewer monster grabbed him and ate him alive. Martino hid from the monster in a pile of wood and junk thrown in the sewer, hatching a bold plan to pass the monster.

Meanwhile, the remaining masked bounty hunters found Manda tied and gagged in the lounge. The black-suited bounty hunter took his mask off. It was Pangera. He removed Manda's gag.

"I'll have you out in a minute," he said. He took out a laser knife and said, "Don't want to burn you with this."

"Careful," said Manda. Pangera used the knife to cut the binds on Manda's wrists and ankles.

Back below in the sewer, Martino grabbed a loose piece of wood and broke it out of its place where built, just in time for the monster to grab him, and so it did. As it tried to eat him, Martino readied the piece of wood and used it to block the monster's jaws. It dropped him. Martino ran toward the place where the monster was being held. He was at a person-sized gateway. The monster turned around. Martino found a switch that activated the massive gate that held the monster in its den. He grabbed a rock and waited for the monster's approach at the large gate. At the right moment, Martino threw the rock at the switch which closed the gate on the monster. The spikes on the closing gate stabbed the monster's back and killed it. Martino went through the person-sized gate and returned to the throne room.

"You have slain my monster," said Owpi. "Perhaps we will make a bargain after all." He looked at his guards and said, "Bring me Captain Tigro and the other freedom fighters!"

Some of the guards held onto Martino as other guards went to the dungeon to grab Tiblo, Skinamar, Regulto, and Steve.

"Master Martino," said the Invisi-Bot, "it's a trick!"

The guards arrived with the other freedom fighters held in the dungeon and then released.

"Tiblo!" said Martino.

"Marty!" said Tiblo as he witnessed him.

"Am I glad to see you?" Martino said.

"Where's Manda?" asked Tiblo.

"I'm right here!" Manda called. She was with the bounty hunter-disguised freedom fighters.

"Pangera!" said Tiblo.

The brown-suited bounty hunter took off her mask. It was Shana.

"Shana!" Tiblo said.

"Very touching!" said Owpi. "The Heavenly Federal freedom fighters together again."

"What should we do with them, sire?" asked the swamp thug called, Glash.

"Let's take them to the Falls of Death!" Owpi commanded.

CHAPTER 6

THE FALLS OF DEATH

Covering the planet was a massive jungle. Apes had been swinging around exploring the place. Large hoofed beasts walked along a path through the jungle.

And so, the freedom fighters were taken on an airship to a massive waterfall that rode down into a crater much like Victoria Falls. Inside the airship, the swamp thugs listened to music as the Invisi-Bot was forced to serve King Owpi as a waiter or butler. The freedom fighters were placed on a hovering platform where Owpi's guards held onto them as the freedom fighters were about to face death over the falls. Soon they were directly over them. The Invisi-Bot gave an announcement speaking out a window of the airship, "His highness says you are to be terminated immediately! And he wants to place the galactic ghost gem in your last nightmares!"

"Invisi-Bot!" Tiblo called to him. "You tell that stupid, abominable pig of hog-smelling crap to do no such thing!"

"Come on, Vizzy, get out of slavery!" shouted Skinamar.

"You pesky heroes will never escape so easily!" said Owpi through another window.

"Owpi!" said Martino. "This is your last chance. Release us . . . or die!"

"Give us the gem and let's be done with it!" shouted Shana.

Owpi laughed. Then he commanded, "Move the human boy into position!"

The guards led Martino to the edge of the hovering platform where there was no fence. Suddenly, a huge, three-headed snake-like monster emerged from the falls and hissed as its large yellow eyes glowed as it stared at the above.

"Drop him!" Owpi commanded.

The guards were about to push Martino off and into the water as he hopped off the edge and grabbed it to hang on. Skinamar found his disk launcher on a nearby shelf with weapons and he stretched his arm to it and pushed it to Martino, allowing it to slide past the guards and across the platform. Martino reached for it and grabbed it. Then he quickly leaped up to fight the guards. The freedom fighters were broken free of their bonds. They fought the guards, grabbed their weapons, and knocked the guards off the platform and they fell into the water. They got eaten by the monster.

A thing with a jet pack flew toward and over the platform. It was Carpoon, the shell-lacking turtle bounty hunter. He landed on the platform within the place where the freedom fighters stood.

"Carpoon!" said Tiblo.

"Yes!" said Carpoon.

The freedom fighters separated as Tiblo faced Carpoon. Pangera leaped off the platform and tried to grab the main airship but fell near the edge of the hole. Martino wanted to get the galactic ghost gem from Owpi. Skinamar helped him by holding him with his feet and stretching his arms out to swing him to the airship. Tiblo pounded Carpoon on the head with one of his blasters. Carpoon fell at the platform's fence.

"Tiblo! Skinamar!" Pangera called as he faced the monster that smelled his flesh and hissed at him. Tiblo leaped down and ran to Pangera as Skinamar followed him as Martino was aboard the ship.

"My leg's broken," said Pangera. The monster approached him as Tiblo held onto his paw. The monster used one of its forked tongues to grab Pangera's foot. Skinamar grabbed Tiblo's feet as he held onto a nearby rubber plant with his feet. Pangera panicked and yelped.

"Skinamar, gimme a gun!" Tiblo said as Skinamar grabbed one of Tiblo's blasters and then gave it to Tiblo. "Don't move, Pangera." Tiblo pointed his blaster at the monster head whose tongue had Pangera and shot it at its nose. The head screamed as it let go of Pangera. Another head hissed and struck toward the heroes as Tiblo shot it. That head screamed, too. The monster went back down into the waterhole.

The remaining freedom fighters were still on the platform. Shana drove it to the airship. They all went aboard as Carpoon awoke. They helped Martino fight Owpi and the swamp thugs. Martino shot his disk launcher at Owpi as he grabbed the galactic ghost gem.

"We gotta get out of here," he said.

Suddenly, the Invisi-Bot showed up and said, "Wait for me!" A thug ran after him. Manda saved him and fought the thug away with her light saber. Martino reached the window. Carpoon showed up.

"Boo!" he said. Martino was frightened. "Give me the gem," said Carpoon.

"You want it?" said Martino. "Get it." He threw it out and the gem fell into the waterhole.

"No!" Carpoon shouted. The gem landed on a rock and it broke. Ghastly fumes vaporized out of it and flew far away. Martino shot Carpoon down and he fell into the hole and the monster ate him.

The freedom fighters fought Owpi until he was down. Guards and thugs were after them until the heroes rejoined and fought the baddies off with a machine gun on the top of the airship. Tiblo found the pilot's cockpit at the front of the deck. He flew the ship where his scouts landed the Great Red Shark. Suddenly, an unexpected visitor flew down from the sky.

CHAPTER 7

REMATCH WITH JOUSTIÁ ÑO

It was Count Joustiáño. He landed in front of the Great Red Shark to challenge the freedom fighters in another battle.

"You've escaped with your captain, I see," he said. "And you let the galactic ghost gem shatter."

"Yeah," said Martino. "That was my fault."

"That means the phantom of the galaxy is free from his eternal prison," said Joustiáño.

"Oh no," said Skinamar, "we're in big trouble."

"Worse," said Shana. "We're gonna be haunted."

"So, freedom fighters," said Joustiáño. "I challenge you once more."

"I don't want to fight you again, Joustiáño," said Tiblo.

"You don't have a choice," Joustiáño said as he lit his light saber. The freedom fighters readied their weapons. The battle started.

As Shana threw her energy-powered boomerang, Joustiáño launched lightning from his fingers and Manda blocked it with an unexpected energy force.

"How did you do that?" asked Shana.

"It must be from Artidector," said Manda.

"Impressive powers you all have," said Joustiáño.

"How about this?" said Martino behind him floating in midair. He had transparent wings that looked like those of Daedalus and Icarus. He fired his disk launcher. Joustiáño quickly blocked it with a force of lightning.

"Since when do we all have super powers?" Skinamar wondered.

Joustiáño spewed fire at Tiblo's shoulder.

"Augh!" Tiblo screamed in pain.

"Artidector taught you well," said Joustiáño. "But he didn't teach you enough." He electrocuted the ground where the freedom fighters stood. Electric walls appeared around them. Joustiáño flew away to his ship.

Pangera showed up as the lightning faded away. "Come on!" he called. "We gotta get back into space."

Everybody climbed aboard the ship and they were flying back into space. A minute later, a call came on the communication system on the dashboard. Tiblo pressed the on button and the hologram of Nala Boomer appeared.

"Boomer here!" she said. "Zinger called me and I'm heading for asteroid 357. Over." The hologram turned off. Tiblo responded.

"We're on our way!" he answered. "Tigro out!" He flew the Great Red Shark to the asteroid that Boomer mentioned.

Meanwhile, on the Death Scale and in the west hangar bay of Serpentopolis. Darth Waternoose awaited the arrival of his master, Emperor Sharp. Count Joustiáño arrived and landed his ship. He flew out of the cockpit and confronted Waternoose.

"The freedom fighters defeated Carpoon and the Phantom of the Galaxy is free," he announced.

"This will be a great battle for the Heaven Federation," said Waternoose. "We may have a chance to win the war."

Joustiáño flew away. Suddenly a shuttle arrived. Guards stepped out on the opening ramp. They set foot on the hangar's metal floor. The emperor had finally arrived; he walked forward and set foot on the floor as well. He walked up to Waternoose and he joined his master into walking.

"My master," said Waternoose. "We have the Death Scale ready for combat once again."

"Excellent, my friend," said the emperor. "The Heaven Federation now no longer stands a chance."

"We shall win the war unless one certain heroine stands up to us," said Waternoose.

"Boomer," said the emperor. "Of course, she wishes to avenge her own death."

"If the freedom fighters fall for our greatest move, we shall be ready for Boomer."

"I'll prepare the welcome for her."

CHAPTER 8

ZINGER'S DEATH

And so, the Heavenly Federal freedom fighters flew to asteroid 357 to meet Zinger. A circular bed was prepared for him. He lay in it.

"Hello, my friends," he said. "I've finally come to my senses. I have to sleep for eternity. It means I have to die."

"Zinger Warsp, you can't die!" said Martino.

"I have no choice," said Zinger. "The many of you have a destiny. You must confront your enemies. There will be a way for you to banish them all simultaneously. And Marty, your sister will live once again."

"Thanks," said Martino.

"I have questions for you, Zinger," said Nala Boomer. "Can you train me once more for my skills?"

"There is no more training to require," said Zinger. "Only one thing remains . . . Waternoose. You must confront Waternoose. But . . . do not underestimate the powers of Emperor Sharp."

"We get the point," said Skinamar.

"Zinger," said Nala. "*Is* Darth Waternoose a dead body from Hawaii?"

Zinger buzzed. He cuddled in the bed.

"Zinger, I must know," said Nala.

"That body *is,*" said Zinger. "There is . . . a . . . word that . . . he used. A special . . . word." He buzzed and suddenly become completely silent. He head lurched aside. And so, Zinger Warsp . . . was finally dead. The bed closed with a glass dome sliding over him and closing shut.

"Don't leave me!" Nala sobbed.

"Miss Boomer," said Tiblo. "Let it go." And so, the freedom fighters started walking back to the ship. Martino gave one last look at Zinger.

"Good bye, Zinger," he said. "Thanks for everything."

Seconds later, the freedom fighters were finally next to the Great Red Shark.

"Who needs him?" said Shana. "We can take on those monsters and bad guys ourselves."

"It's gonna be our ultimate challenge," said Skinamar.

"I can't do it," said Nala.

"Huh?" said Martino.

"I can't fight Waternoose," Nala said. "It's just—without Zinger . . ."

"I know how you feel," said Martino.

Suddenly, a white column appeared among the heroes.

CHAPTER 9

ARTIDECTOR'S BOON

"Zinger will always be with you," it was Artidector.

"Artidector!" said all the freedom fighters.

"Are we glad to see you?" said Skinamar.

"Why didn't you tell me before?" Nala asked Artidector. "You told me that the Serpentials consumed a dead body from Hawaii."

"That body," Artidector explained, "was once a man named, Keanu Bonula. He was a hero for his home island, who fought evil invaders trying to immigrate. I was with him those many years ago when I was a mortal. A prophecy was foretold that if one hero dies, he will have a new life of evil.

"You see, Nala, what I said was true. The Serpentials not actually consumed it by devouring it. They used it to create an advisory apprentice for Emperor Sharp. And so, he was put within a mechanical body named, Waternoose.

I thought I could protect Keanu from that prophecy as well as I protected other heroes. But I was wrong."

"But why would they steal a dead body?" asked Martino.

"It's like Frankenstein," said Skinamar.

"How can I fight him?" asked Nala to Artidector.

"He is more machine than human," said Artidector. "If you have vengeance for your original death, you can conquer the enemies of your past."

"But I can't do it," said Nala.

"You must try," said Artidector. "Control your fear and temper. You must have strength and courage."

"I can't kill someone who was once dead."

"Then the emperor has already won."

"He's right you know," said Skinamar.

"Everything depends on all of you," said Artidector. "Any evil can be stopped by any heroes."

"And one more thing," said Martino. "The galactic ghost gem has shattered. The phantom of the galaxy is free from his prison."

"That is one mighty enemy," said Artidector. "Brain Tentacles wanted to conquer the universe with that phantom, but . . . now he will lose to that situation."

"Thank you, Artidector," said Martino.

The Great Red Shark's entrance door opened. The ramp was set on the asteroid's surface. The freedom fighters climbed aboard, while Nala Boomer hopped into her own fighter ship. Everyone one was ready to fly back to the Heaven Federation's current base.

Chapter 10

The Madness of Brain Tentacles

The Heaven Federation's current base was a space station floating in the center of an asteroid field. The Forbidden UFO approached the station. Inside the UFO, Brain Tentacles looked at a displayed hologram of his wife. He shed tears as he remembered her dying from a poisonous alien. He switched off the projector and felt angry that he could not get his appendages on the galactic ghost gem. The UFO's hangar made contact with the station's hangar. The mutant mixed aliens entered the station. Brain Tentacles approached the commanding officers' offices.

"They will be sorry," he said.

Just then General Grizzle appeared to confront him.

"You let your freedom fighters steal the gem I wanted," said Brain Tentacles.

"I-I don't know what you mean," said the general.

"Don't lie to me!" Brain Tentacles snapped.

"Um . . ." said the general, "my captain has the answer. He told me the gem has broken."

"What?!?"

The mixed aliens arrived. Brain Tentacles ordered, "Attack!" The aliens took on every officer one by one. A new member of the band was called, Squirmwarg, a metal-bodied alien with a magma worm for a head that squirms out of the body's head socket. The worm was covered in red shingle-like scales; it had three glowing yellow eyes, and a frill with paddle-like fins. Squirmwarg approached the general and struck at him with his magma worm head. The general backed away.

Meanwhile, the other aliens had sabotaged the station's power system. Everything was a black out. Brain Tentacles held an officer and he plunged his tongues into his nose and mouth, and he tortured him with his tentacle beard. Then he dropped him. He walked back to General Grizzle.

"We shall meet again for the final time, General Grizzle," said Brain Tentacles. And so, he walked away with his followers.

As soon as the aliens boarded back on the Forbidden UFO, the station was filled with random colors of slime from green to purple to brown to black. Knowing that all communication lines were dead, the general realized that he had to wait for the freedom fighters to return.

Chapter 11

Operation Blue Star

Right on schedule, the freedom fighters arrived. As they walked off the Great Red Shark, they found out that the whole station was blacked out.

"What happened?" asked Martino.

"Beats me," said Tiblo. He took out his laser knife and turned it on.

"Anybody have a light?" asked Regulto.

"I got one," said Skinamar. He took out a torch that was held in his backpack. Then he turned it on. The freedom fighters walked down the halls to look for clues.

"Slime!" Skinamar exclaimed as he shone his torch on a wall of slime.

"Brain Tentacles has been here," said Manda.

"Looks like he and his goons must have sabotaged the power system," said Martino.

"That's what we're gonna find out," said Tiblo. He activated his wrist communicator and tried contacting one of the Heavenly Federal officers. He made contact with General Grizzle. The general's hologram appeared.

"General Grizzle here!" he said. "Captain Tigro, our station has been invaded by Brain Tentacles."

"That's what we all figured," said Tiblo. "I believe his goons sabotaged the power here."

"That is correct," said the general. "The best amount of power is a drop of a star flare. Come to my office. I have a device for that."

"We're on our way," said Tiblo. "Captain Tigro out." He turned off his communicator.

And so, the freedom fighters walked to the general's office. As they arrived, the general showed them a strange, hose-like device coiled in a square rack.

"This device will help gather the power we need," the general explained. "Point it at a tiny particle of a star flare and it will absorb energy." The device had a point that looked like an antenna on the very end.

"It's almost like watering my uncle's garden," said Martino.

"Use it wisely," said the general. "The best place is near a blue star."

"But those are the hottest stars ever," said Martino.

"We'll get burned to a crisp," said Skinamar.

"All you must do is stay back from the star," the general explained, "extend the line toward one flare and when the power is caught then reel it in like a fishing rod."

"Thanks," said Martino.

"We'll be back as soon as the power is ours," said Tiblo.

And so, the freedom fighters left the office and walked back to the hangar bay.

"How are we going to survive this?" asked Shana.

"It'll be worth our best shot," said Martino. They all boarded the Great Red Shark. Tiblo started the engine and flew out of the hangar. Meanwhile, Pangera watched the ship leave. He was about to become a Heavenly Federal officer.

As the freedom fighters flew through space, Tiblo used scanners to find the nearest blue star. He flew the ship in the direction of the nearest stars and sped the ship at full throttle. And so, they were near a blue star.

"Here it is," said Tiblo. "Somebody has to get dressed for the outside."

Martino and Manda volunteered. They each put on a space suit. They grabbed the power collecting device and headed for the lower deck. A hatch ahead of the ship's deck opened and Martino carried the hose while Manda held the rack.

"I gotta make it close enough," said Martino as he jumped into space with the hose. He floated toward the star. He drew the hose closer to a flare. It took him five minutes to make it long enough and close to one flare.

"He's almost got it!" said Skinamar as he watched out the window. Suddenly, the point of the hose was touched by one flare. The point burned bright yellow and Martino pulled it back.

"Yes!" he shouted. "Quick get me out of here!" he called to the others. Manda pulled in the hose as Martino held on. She pulled it and him all the way in by holding the rack and stepping backward toward the up way. Soon the heroes were back together. Tiblo flew the ship back to station.

A while later, the station's power was restored and lights were shining bright and new. The freedom fighters were congratulated. And also, the alien slime was cleaned away.

CHAPTER 12

THE STRATEGY

An assembly was settled in the strategy room. There appeared many different animals in the Heaven Federation. There were also friendly aliens sitting in seats of the room. The freedom fighters looked for seats and Tiblo bumped into Pangera, who was wearing a new suit with a badge and star pins.

"Wow, look at you," said Tiblo.

"I'm a commodore admiral," said Pangera.

"Good for you," said Tiblo. He patted Pangera on his side. "Good luck with it."

And so, everyone was seated. The strategy table showed a hologram of the Death Scale next to a tropical planet. General Grizzle announced, "The Death Scale, now back together, has moved to a planet for orbiting. It is carrying a shield. The emperor has ordered his elite forces to guard a generator hidden in a bunker on the planet Sorina. Admiral Wolfgang, proceed."

Admiral Wanko Wolfgang continued the announcement pointing at different sections of the hologram, "You can see here, the Death Scale hovers over the planet meeting with the energy that activates the shield around. To end this war, we must destroy this biosphere once and for all. First, the shield must be deactivated. After it is down, then we must enter a crack by the volcanoes known as Mount Blazer and its sons and then follow the way down the crevice . . ." the hologram showed the inside of the Death Scale with tunnels leading to its power core. ". . . and through one of these tunnels and into the core and firing at it. Once the core is shot down, it will explode and that should destroy the Death Scale once and for all." The hologram of the Death Scale flashed a white and blue light and disappeared.

"Excellent, Admiral," said the general. "Now we need one team on the planet and another team flying in space to enter the Death Scale's core."

"I'm with you!" called out Nala Boomer walking among the seats.

"She'll be with us," said Tiblo.

"Class dismissed," said the admiral. All the Heavenly Federal pilots and soldiers, along with the freedom fighters headed for the hangar bay, where many ships were all prepared and ready for the mission. Tiblo spoke with Pangera as they stood next to the Great Red Shark.

"By the way, Pangera," said Tiblo, "the Shark's all yours if you want it back."

"I let you have it," said Pangera, "so, why not keep it?"

"I just want you to know that you've been a good friend to me," Tiblo said.

"All right," said Pangera. "I'll recruit some pilots."

The freedom fighters' ships were driven out of the Great Red Shark's hangar bay. They stood next to them. Tiblo went to his ship. And so, all the pilots were set in their cockpits. General Grizzle had to fly a shuttle with soldiers for fighting on the planet for finding the Death Scale's shield bunker. The freedom fighters flew in their fighter ships and followed the general's shuttle out of the hangar bay. They all activated the hyper-drive system of each ship. And they were off to planet Sorina.

Moments passed. The soldiers and freedom fighters started to enter the orbit as a Serpential scale carrier moved by. Inside that ship, Waternoose approached some officers sitting behind a control board.

"Where are those ships going?" asked Waternoose.

"I'll check their status," said Commander Karbono Kassow. He pressed a button to contact the freedom fighters and soldiers with a loudspeaker: "Where are you headed, fine intruders?"

General Grizzle answered, "We're approaching planet Sorina to land there with troops on a mission."

"Very well," said Commander Kassow.

"As I predicted," said Waternoose. "Nala Boomer is with them. I have sought it with my chronic vision."

In the group of ships headed for the planet, Nala knew about the carrier with a strange feeling.

"Waternoose is on that ship," she said.

"It's just your imagination," said Tiblo. "We're almost there."

"I can feel it," said Nala. As the heroes continued their voyage, the Serpential officers had an announcement for their strategy.

"We have elite troopers waiting for the Heaven Federation," said Captain Kerbano Kassow.

"Excellent," said Waternoose. "Allow the enemy to survive until our time to battle. My master will be pleased to see Boomer."

And so, the soldiers and freedom fighters finally landed their ships on the planet's surface. They readied their weapons, preparing for combat as they set up camp.

Chapter 13

Planet Sorina

After the moment of landing and setting up camp, the freedom fighters and soldiers explored the jungles of the planet in search of any activity from the enemy. Meanwhile, Serpential troopers had the exact same idea. The new elite troopers were dressed in unique uniforms: Gecko troopers are geckos with hooded helmets. Camou troopers are chameleons in uniforms of their shape. Igu troopers are iguanas. And draco troopers are Komodo dragons or bearded dragons in dark gray suits with jet packs. Also the camou troopers have the ability to camouflage within the environment, and the igu troopers can slice around with spikes and blades on their spines.

And so, the Heavenly Federal soldiers took various steps across the tall grass of the jungle nearby.

"Hold your position," commanded General Grizzle.

"There can be life on this planet," said Tiblo.

"Perhaps they're intelligent," said Manda.

"So, General," said a male canine soldier, "do you suppose the enemy will be ready for us by now."

"They and we will be ready whenever," said the general.

The freedom fighters walked ahead a few yards and found the camp of the elite troopers. They had speeders next to their stations.

"I see some Serpential troopers with a large chest over there," said Martino.

"This could be dangerous," said Tiblo.

"Can you investigate?" said Martino. "Tigers can face danger, right? So try to get a better look."

"Hey," said Tiblo in a sense of humor. "It's me." He went to seek the chest.

Suddenly, a draco trooper caught Tiblo sneaking toward their camp. An igu trooper opened the chest and large mosquitoes emerged into the air.

"Flu-bugs!" Tiblo shouted as he ran back to the others. "Serpential insects that spread a contagious disease."

The troopers grabbed guns and started to fire at the freedom fighters. They fought the flu-bugs by firing at them over their heads. Suddenly, the troopers started the engines on their speeders. Heavenly Federal soldiers had speeders, too. They gave the freedom fighters rides on the back of each seat. A chase was on.

Chapter 14

Jungle Chase

Racing through the jungle were speeders about to fight and smash each other into smoldering wreckage. Heavenly Federal soldiers gave the freedom fighters speeders. Tiblo, Martino, and Manda rode on some as troopers chased them through the jungle.

As Martino and Manda zoomed ahead, Tiblo decided to take care of two troopers behind them. He bumped into each of them at his sides. He later jumped on one of them and covered a trooper's face for ten seconds until they met a tree. Tiblo jumped away as the trooper crashed.

Martino and Manda were ahead as more troopers on speeders came by. Manda decided to head for a cave under a rock.

"Are you crazy, Manda?!" Martino shouted.

"I'm trying to hide!" Manda said as she went into the cave and a trooper chased her. She fell on the ground as the trooper chased the empty speeder. Manda lit her saber at the trooper's speeder. The speeder spun football-style and crashed into a stone wall.

Martino was still being chased. He grabbed a hanging jungle vine. The trooper watched him and suddenly crashed without looking. Martino let go of the vine and landed back on the ground.

"I gotta get back to Tiblo and the others," he said. He headed back for the other freedom fighters.

Chapter 15

Waternoose's Message

Meanwhile, Darth Waternoose flew a ship back to the Death Scale and walked to the Palace of Sharp. He went there to report to his master. He walked up the stairs of the throne room. Emperor Sharp looked out his rear window for any sign of the enemy Starfleet. Hooker and Blunt Volton (the twin brother vulture viceroys) flew down and saluted for Waternoose's presence as he approached near the throne.

"I ordered you to remain on the command ship," said the emperor.

"I have sensed the presence of the Heavenly Federal freedom fighters," said Waternoose. "Nala Boomer is with them."

"Ah," said the emperor. "So she is."

"This is gonna be good, Hooker," said Blunt.

"We're gonna see that Boomer again," said Hooker.

"Bring me Nala Boomer," said the emperor to Waternoose. "Together we can teach her the ways of our empire. She will repent to the Serpent's Ghost. I've waited a long time for this moment."

"As you wish," said Waternoose. He walked out of the throne room and headed back to the ship he flew on. The emperor hissed, flicking his forked tongue. Waternoose headed for Sorina to land on a base built on it.

Chapter 16

The Mingklins

Back on the planet, Manda rested inside the cave for twenty minutes. As that happened, a strange creature that looked like a kangaroo-hopping dragon about the size of a chimpanzee, hauled over to Manda. It nudged its snout at her hip. It repeatedly tapped it there. Suddenly, Manda awoke from her nap.

"Cut it out!" she said as she found the creature staring face to face. "Hello. Are you lost?"

The creature spoke its language with many tongue taps and palate snaps. Manda stood up against the cave's wall.

"Want something to eat?" she asked the creature. She dug into her pack for some food supply. She found a small package of bacon. "Here," she gave one strip to the creature. "Eat it." The creature opened its mouth and nibbled on the bacon strip.

"Do you have a name?" Manda asked the creature again.

"Rat'la," the creature said.

"You have small horns," Manda studied the creature with much of her heart. The creature was pink with flat feet like a rabbit. "You must be a female." Manda sensed the creature and finished studying it.

Rat'la found Manda's light saber lying on the cave's floor. She tried grabbing it with her small Parasaurolophus-like hands and Manda stopped her.

"Don't touch that," she said. "That's dangerous." She put it in a loop on her belt. "It's for *me* to use." She patted on it. "Come on. Let's get out of here." She led the way out of the cave as Rat'la followed her.

Suddenly, Rat'la heard a sound with her cow-like ears creeping through the jungle. A blaster shot emerged right by the cave's entrance. Manda and Rat'la leaped back in the cave. Manda lit her saber for any emergency. Another blaster shot came. Manda turned her saber off and squatted to the ground lying flat on her front.

"Freeze!" a microphonic voice came from above.

"Augh!" Manda screamed. She found where the voice came from was a gecko trooper standing by her.

"Get up!" said the trooper. He turned to another trooper and said, "Get your ride. Take her to base." The distant trooper went to get his speeder. Suddenly, Rat'la attacked the standing trooper at his feet.

"What the—?" he said. Manda lit her saber and slashed the trooper away. The trooper's suit was torn and much blood spilt. It took 10 seconds to heal as Manda and

Rat'la escaped. They ran from the cave to a bush in the jungle. They hid from any more threats happening around.

"Where did you come from?" Manda asked Rat'la. Rat'la spoke her tongue and led the way for Manda to follow.

Meanwhile, Martino rejoined the others.

"Where's Manda?" asked Tiblo.

"We got separated," said Martino.

"We must find her," said Tiblo. "She could be lost."

"Talk about a safari," said Skinamar.

"This place gives me the creeps," said Shana.

"This is just like the good ol' days in Australia," said Steve Irwin. The freedom fighters walked through the jungle in search of Manda.

"Be not afraid," Rufus the beast's voice growled inside Regulto's mind. Regulto concentrated on being brave as everyone walked through.

A moment later, Regulto found a strange item, a wooden scarecrow with a dead furry animal's hide.

"Hey!" he called to the others. "Over here!"

"What is it, Reg?" asked Tiblo.

"A dead animal hide on a scarecrow," said Regulto as he studied it, "hunted by primitives. Its hide is used to decorate this artifact."

"Impressive," said Tiblo.

"Crikey," said Steve. "A trophy."

"We better not touch it," said Martino. They all went up to the scarecrow.

"It must be a decoration of some kind," said Tiblo.

"I say it's a prize of money matters," said Steve as he reached for the animal hide.

"Steve, wait! NO!" Tiblo shouted. Steve touched the scarecrow and suddenly, a large net rose from under their feet and the freedom fighters were caught in a trap.

"Look at the size of this net!" said Shana.

"Vines and shrubs," said Skinamar.

"Fine mess we're in," said Tiblo. "Great, Steve! Always living in the past thinking of your former career."

"Will everybody relax, so I can get us out of here?" said Martino. "Tiblo, can I borrow your laser knife?"

"Sure," said Tiblo struggling to reach his pocket. "I'll get it." He reached his hip pocket to get his knife. He barely got it and tried reaching for Martino's hand, which was free through a hole. Martino got the knife from Tiblo and started cutting the net by turning it on. He sliced every bar of vine around him until everybody fell back on solid ground.

"I always land on my feet," said Shana.

"Man, I feel broken," said Martino. The laser knife was turned off when they fell.

"Nice going, Marty," said Tiblo. "I always land on all fours."

"You're even a better hero than I was," said Nala.

Suddenly, clapping and waving plants surrounded the heroes.

"We've got company," said Skinamar.

"I hate this," said Regulto.

Around the plants were hopping, kangaroo-like dragons the size of chimpanzees with banana-shaped horns. Colors of their skins included blue, green, purple, and pink. These creatures were the same kind as Rat'la.

"Little hopping dragons," said Shana.

"Perhaps I can calculate some research," said the Invisi-Bot.

A blue creature with rubbery whiskers and large goat horns held a spear and pointed it at Tiblo, speaking its language.

"Hey," said Tiblo. "Point that thing away from me." He said, moving the spear aside. The creature spoke more of its language and pointed the spear at Tiblo again.

"Hey!" Tiblo grabbed the spear harshly.

"Tiblo," said Martino. "Don't."

All the creatures spread their hands out and started kneeling, then rising, then kneeling and rising repeatedly and slowly before the Invisi-Bot.

"What are they doing?" asked Shana.

"Well," said the Invisi-Bot. "It appears that they think I am some sort of god."

"O-ooh!" the creatures moaned as they repented.

"Ah!" the Invisi-Bot came to a sense as he started beeping and receiving research of the creatures. "Now, I'm getting a reading. These creatures are called 'Mingklins'. They are a very young specimen. Their language appears to have no soft consonants, which is why they tap their tongues and clap them with their mouths. Quite primitive, aren't they?"

Some of the Mingklins built a chair for the Invisi-Bot and carried him into it. Others tied the heroes to wooden branches with thick vines and everybody was being carried away from the spot.

"Haven't you finished that translator yet, Shana?" asked Martino.

"I'm almost done with it," said Shana. "I need more time to work on it as soon as we reach a stop spot."

CHAPTER 17

THE MINGKLIN VILLAGE

And so, the Mingklins carried the freedom fighters to their village. It was a magnificent place with tree houses, climbing ropes, agricultural products, and wooden carts and wagons.

"What a delicate place you fellows have," the Invisi-Bot said to the Mingklins.

The big-horned, whiskered, blue Mingklin, Chief Grok, spoke his language to him as they all crossed a rickety bridge from a cliff top to the nearest wood-built balcony on a tree.

"More readings!" said the Invisi-Bot studying the Mingklins and their place. "The big-horned ones are males while the small-horned ones are females."

"Wonderful access you have," said Shana.

"I'm getting the whole idea of this, it's interesting," said Martino.

"Me, too," said Skinamar.

The Mingklins carried them from balcony to balcony across every bridge in their path.

"It's almost like Fern Gully," said Skinamar.

"That farm down there reminds me of my uncle's garden," said Martino as he found a Mingklin growing crops below.

The Mingklins carried the heroes to the biggest tree house in the village. The house belonged to the chief. Manda appeared through the entrance with leaf-woven curtains. She was dressed in a green fur dress decorated with tall grass.

"Manda!" said Martino and Shana simultaneously.

"Manda!" said Tiblo.

"Mistress Manda Monka!" said the Invisi-Bot.

The Mingklins guarded Manda's path by stopping her with the points of spears. They spoke their language.

"But these are my friends," Manda said. "Invisi-Bot, tell them to release them."

"I'm sorry," said the Invisi-Bot. "My electronic brain is still downloading research of this new specimen."

"Can you speak their language?" asked Martino.

"C'mon, Vizzy, I'm tired of hanging around all day," said Skinamar.

"Why don't you try using your language banks and get us out of this?" said Tiblo.

"I'll try," said the Invisi-Bot. He started speaking the Mingklins' language to them. He tried to order the Mingklins to release the freedom fighters. Suddenly, the chief hard an insult from him and pointed his spear and scolded at him.

"Well, excuse me!" the Invisi-Bot said and leaned back in the wooden chair almost about to fall off the balcony. "WHOA!" he shouted. The Mingklins helped him up. Then the Invisi-Bot was up right. Rat'la appeared next to the chief and convinced him into releasing the heroes.

"Oh, thank you," said the Invisi-Bot to the Mingklins. "I almost died . . . or fell into scrap by the way."

Chief Grok agreed with Rat'la and ordered the orders to release the freedom fighters. The Mingklins cut their bonds with knives made of stone. Sooner or later, the heroes were free to walk anywhere to explore the village and interact with the Mingklins, introducing themselves. Shana finally finished working on the translator for all the freedom fighters' communicators.

And so, night arrived. The Invisi-Bot told the Mingklins the whole story about himself and the freedom fighters fighting against the Serpential forces. The freedom fighters looked around the village as Mingklins lit torches and beacons with fire for the night.

"Isn't this place beautiful?" asked Manda.

"Yeah, it's great," said Martino.

"Fantastic," said Skinamar.

"I was worried about you, Manda," said Tiblo.

"Well at least we made some new friends," said Manda.

"I better check on the Invisi-Bot," said Shana. She hopped to the chief's house. Inside, the Invisi-Bot was getting to the end of his story as the others followed Shana to that house. They all looked through the window. The chief prepared a campfire and the Mingklins danced around it.

"Marvelous," said the Invisi-Bot. He turned to the freedom fighters and said, "We are now part of the tribe."

As the heroes watched the Mingklins dance, they all entered the house to stay warm by the fire—except for Nala Boomer. She went by a balcony to think about her destiny.

CHAPTER 18

NALA BOOMER'S DESTINY

Nala looked at herself and thought about her previous life and her current life. A cold air passed within the trees as she felt it on her face. Martino and Manda found her standing and leaning on the fence. They walked up to her and began to talk.

"What's up?" asked Martino.

"Do you guys remember what Zinger said?" Nala asked the others.

"Of course," said Martino.

"Whatever he told you, you don't have to do it," said Manda.

"Yes I do," Nala sighed.

"We all know your story," said Martino. "You were captured and executed."

"Artidector brought me back to life for this one thing," Nala explained. "Waternoose is here. I can sense it. I must face him in battle. That's why I have to go."

"How can you face him alone?" asked Manda. "You have feelings that we don't understand. You can never fight him and live."

"I have a new zorcher with me," said Nala.

"Why are you to face him?" asked Martino.

"Because . . ." said Nala, ". . . like Zinger said, he was once a historical hero from Hawaii."

"A hero??" said Manda.

"From Hawaii??" said Martino.

"Yes," said Nala. "If I have a chance I can help remember his previous life and turn him back."

"You'll run away," said Manda, "*far* away. If that is your task then leave this place."

"Good luck, Nala," said Martino. "It's nice knowing you."

"I have to try," said Nala. "I hope Skinamar took care of you as well as he took care of me."

"Yeah," said Martino.

Nala left the place and walked along bridges and balconies until she was out of the village and seen no more.

"Hey!" a voice called to Martino and Manda. It was Tiblo walking toward them. "What's going on here?"

"Nothing," said Manda.

"Everything's fine," said Martino. "We just had a talk with Nala and she left us."

"I just want to be alone for a while," said Manda, "just to catch some fresh, cold air."

"Nothing??" said Tiblo.

"Nala said she has to face her destiny," said Martino.

"I see," said Tiblo. Martino walked back to the Mingklin chief's house as Tiblo walked to where Manda leaned on the balcony's fence.

"Hey, Manda, what's the matter with you?" he asked.

Manda turned to him and felt shy as she said, "I-I . . . I can't tell you."

Tiblo looked around and said, "Could you tell Marty, is that who you can tell?" He pointed toward the chief's house.

"It's something about my father," said Manda. "Brain Tentacles. Hold me." She hugged Tiblo as he hugged her, too.

"It's alright," he said.

"We all have a destiny, don't we?" said Manda. Tiblo patted her back.

And so, Nala traveled through the jungle to where she was supposed to go. A hangar was set up days before by the Serpentials. A shuttle was waiting on the tarmac on top. Waternoose was walking off of it and riding down the nearest elevator as he waited for Nala Boomer. Meanwhile, Nala was caught by a security system and scale troopers caught her and put her in brass binders and they took her to the hangar to show her to Waternoose. Waternoose waited on a balcony until an elevator arrived with Commander Karbono Kassow and the scale troopers with Nala captured.

"My lord," said the commander. "This lioness has snooped toward our hangar and we found her. She was armed only with this." He held up his wing with a new zorcher that Nala carried with her, showing it to Waternoose. Waternoose grabbed the zorcher and looked at it.

"Good work, commander," he said. "Leave her with me."

"As you wish," said the commander as he rode with the troopers on the elevator to a higher level. Darth Waternoose and Nala Boomer walked along the balcony next to each other.

"The emperor has been expecting you," said Waternoose.

"I know . . ." said Nala, "should I say 'Mr. Bonula'."

"So," said Waternoose as he quickly turned his head at Nala. "I sense you have accepted the truth."

"I accepted the truth that you were once a man named, Keanu Bonula, from Hawaii," Nala explained.

"That name," Waternoose put his hand with Nala's zorcher up in front of her, "no longer has any meaning for me. And so, it is obvious you cannot turn me back."

"But I sensed one part of you that is still good." Nala leaned on a fence with her bound paws under her chin. "If you just look deep within yourself, you might understand something."

Waternoose studied Nala's new zorcher and pressed the trigger to fire a V-shape of white energy from two spines on the front of its muzzle. The energy hit a distant tree.

"I see you have constructed a new zorcher," said Waternoose. "Your skills are complete." He switched the zorcher's power off. "Indeed you are skillful with an amount of power. The emperor has foreseen it."

"Come with me," said Nala. "Perhaps I can remind you of what being a hero was like for you."

"I have no right for that now," said Waternoose. "You don't know the power of the Serpent's Ghost. I must obey my master. The emperor will be pleased to see your skills. He is your master now."

"If you let go of your hate," said Nala, "maybe you'll understand the truth I have told you."

"It is too late for me, Nala."

Scale troopers came by and surrounded Nala.

"Then there is no Keanu Bonula," she said.

"Take her up to the tarmac where she'll be waiting for me," Waternoose commanded the troopers.

"Yes, sir," one of the troopers said as they did what Waternoose said. He started to think of what he and Nala discussed until he walked to another elevator to follow the way up to the top.

CHAPTER 19

THE WAR BEGINS

The next morning arrived after Nala Boomer and Darth Waternoose flew on a shuttle to the Death Scale. The remaining heroes had a plan to sneak into the shield bunker by passing the troopers guarding the entrance. Three gecko troopers showed up by the bunker with speeders, one for each trooper.

"All we must do is sneak into the bunker," said Tiblo, "with a diversion of some kind." A green male Mingklin hopped to the speeders.

"There goes Guk," said Martino. The Mingklin called, Guk, stole one of the speeders and started it. He zoomed away with it.

"Hey!" one of the troopers shouted. Two of them got on their speeders and chased after Guk.

"Not bad for the little guy, there's only one left," said Tiblo. "Well, that's our cue." The freedom fighters walked to the bunker and fought off the remaining trooper. In the meantime, Guk and the two troopers raced through the jungle. Guk did tricks on the speeder, taunting the troopers as they approached him. As one trooper was close to him, Guk kicked him aside with his two feet about a yard away. The trooper looked ahead and saw a tree stump. He crashed into it and his speeder exploded. Guk stood on the speeder by his hands on the handlebars.

"Woo-hoo!" he shouted. He rested back on the seat. "Hoo-kee-dih-bah," he spoke in his own tongue, taunting.

The remaining trooper hovered behind him. Guk looked ahead and saw a vine. He grabbed it as he let go of the speeder. The trooper chased it until he crashed into a tree exploding with it.

Meanwhile, back at the bunker, Tiblo made contact with the Heavenly Federal forces.

"This is Captain Tigro," he said through his communicator. "My scouts and I are at the bunker." The leading officers received that message. Admiral Wolfgang commanded all spacecraft to travel to the orbit of Sorina. All ships, including the mothership, activated the hyper-drive system in each craft. Very soon, the Heavenly Federal forces zoomed into distant space at light speed. They were finally on their way.

CHAPTER 20

VISITING THE EMPEROR

And so, Nala and Waternoose flew to the Death Scale and into Serpentopolis. They walked to the Palace of Sharp then rode the elevator up to the throne room to meet the emperor. They walked off the elevator as it made its stop. The guards standing on each side of the shaft found them. As they saw Waternoose, they hailed to him and stood at their posts. Nala and Waternoose walked up the stairs to face Emperor Sharp. The emperor sat in his throne, looking out the back window. He pressed a button that rotated his throne around to face Nala and Waternoose.

"Welcome, Nala Boomer," he said, hissing. "I have been expecting you." He flicked his forked tongue. "You no longer need those." He pointed his finger at the binder cuffs around Nala's paws. They were unlocked with a secret force. They fell to the ground. Nala looked at her paws being free. The emperor chuckled.

"Guards, leave us!" he commanded the guards at the elevator. They each walked one direction away from the elevator. They were out of the emperor's sight.

"I hear that you have become very powerful and skillful as I have foreseen it," the emperor said to Nala.

"Your powers have no effect on me and now I am yet a brave fighter," said Nala.

"Oh no," said the emperor, as he stood up off his throne. He walked toward Nala and Waternoose. "My powers will perhaps turn you over to my empire. And I won't have to execute you like before."

"Her zorcher," said Waternoose as he showed his master Nala's zorcher.

The emperor grabbed it and said, "Ah yes. A freedom fighter's weapon." He walked back to his throne with it. "Soon the empire will be strong with more advanced weapons." He sat down. "Your Heaven Federation shall not stand one chance against it. Oh and . . . I'm afraid this biosphere will be quite operational when your friends arrive."

Chapter 21

Inside The Bunker

The freedom fighters on the planet surface cracked the code to the shield bunker's entrance. Serpential officers guarded the place. Tiblo put up one of his blasters and shouted, "Alright! Everybody step aside." The officers did what he said. They all stepped away from the heroes' path with their hands up.

"Quickly, quickly," said Tiblo. "Now you must all leave. We're taking over!"

"Don't count on it!" shouted a large lizard pirate knight.

Skinamar grabbed a large piece of scrap metal and threw it at that knight. The knight screamed and fell over the fence and down in the power generation system.

"Halt!" shouted some troopers. A draco and an igu and some camou troopers surrounded the freedom fighters.

"How unfair," said Shana.

"They always catch us red-handed," said Tiblo.

"It happens," said Skinamar. The heroes all put their hands up as the troopers pointed their guns at them. They turned them to a Komodo dragon officer.

"You Heavenly Federal scum," said the officer frowning at them.

CHAPTER 22

STARFLEET STRUGGLE

The Heavenly Federal forces arrived near Sorina, confronting the planet. The power was switched off for the hyper-drive. Admiral Wolfgang commanded the starfleet.

"Choose a target!" he said. "Fire on as many pirate knights as you can!" Numerous pirate knight fighter ships surrounded the Heavenly Federal pilots.

"There are too many of them!" said a canine pilot.

Pangera Pelwoski flew the Great Red Shark with random animals and aliens.

"We must be in big trouble, Commodore," said an owl in the seat next to the pilot.

"Don't worry," said Pangera. "I'll get us out of this." He turned back to some blue, black-nosed aliens firing the Shark's guns. "Fire on all surroundings!"

The aliens responded, speaking their language as they shot down many pirate knight ships.

Inside the Palace of Sharp, the emperor showed Nala Boomer the large window behind his throne and pointed to the right.

"Go on, my new apprentice," he said. "See for yourself."

Nala walked up a small staircase up to a window where she found the Heaven Federation fight against a large number of Serpential fighters that defended the Death Scale.

"Nobody stands a chance against my empire now," said the emperor. "You will soon face the end of your insignificant Heaven Federation."

Nala looked at the emperor and then found her zorcher on the right arm of the throne. The emperor set his clawed hand over it.

"You want this," he said, "don't you? Go ahead, take your weapon and shoot me down with all your hatred. It will help complete your vengeance for the end of your previous life."

"No," said Nala.

The emperor laughed, hissed, and chuckled. "It is unavoidable," he said. "You know you have no other choice. It is your destiny. You . . . like the dead man I stole . . . are now . . . mine!" Nala took another look out the window.

CHAPTER 23

MINGKLIN WARFARE

Back on the planet surface, the freedom fighters led some Serpentials out of the bunker. Afterwards, Tiblo snuck behind a gecko trooper and patted his shoulder. Then Tiblo ran to a place nearby.

"Hey!" shouted the trooper. He followed Tiblo to a group of Heavenly Federal soldiers for a surprise attack. They shot the trooper down.

Suddenly, the Mingklins surprised the enemy force with weapons and heavy artillery. Many of them swung on vines and jumped on some troopers. Pirate knights and some officers rode in two-legged, lizard-headed walkers. They fired blasters in front to cause destruction of the jungle. Mingklins fired one of their wooden catapults at a walker nearby. The rocks dented it and the walker turned around and fired its blasters at the catapult. The Mingklins ran off. In the jungle, the Mingklins had slings with which they flung rocks at troopers and pirate knights. Rat'la tried swinging a sling and she smacked herself in the face with it. One blue male Mingklin flew through the air on a glider among trees and held vines holding rocks on his fingers and wrists. He dropped on rock at a time on top of each trooper or pirate knight he flew over. He dropped a rock on a scale trooper and as that trooper fell to the ground, he unexpectedly shot his blaster up at the glider's wing. The Mingklin slowly swiveled and fell to the ground.

CHAPTER 24

OPERATIONAL BIOSPHERE

In space, Heavenly Federal pilots fought with pirate knights in fighter ships. Many Heavenly Federal pilots were shot down. A leader pilot said, “Keep track of your targets.”

A male feline pilot shot a pirate knight down. “Got him!” he said.

“Good shot, Paxton!” said another leader pilot.

In the Great Red Shark, the owl panicked about dying friends and allies.

“I say we fly down for shelter and later make a special strike,” he said.

“Take it easy, my friend’s down there,” said Pangera.

A pilot was shot by a fast moving pirate knight ship. “I’m HIT!” he shouted. Then his ship burned and he crashed on top of a scale cruiser.

Nala Boomer watched the battle outside the window of the throne room of the Palace of Sharp.

"You see, my young apprentice," said Emperor Sharp, "your friends have failed." Nala turned her face to him and the emperor said, "Now . . . time to meet our newly equipped and operational biosphere." He pressed a button on the arm of his throne and spoke through the communication system, "Fire at will, commander."

And so, in the basement, officers activated the Death Scale's firing system, pressing every button and pulling every lever and switch. Much of the power of Serpentopolis was used. The spires at the end of each building fired lasers at the mechanical serpent's eye at the top of the palace and the eye absorbed the beams and shot a larger beam at one of the Heaven Federation's motherships. It exploded into smoldering sparks of metal and a small section of it remained, floating through space.

"The blast came from the Death Scale," said Pangera. "That thing's operational."

"Commodore Pelwoski!" the admiral contacted him. "Lead the pilots away until our soldiers take out the shield."

"I'm doing my best, Admiral," said Pangera. "I'm losing a bit much."

"We're all gonna die, Commodore!" said the owl chattering in fear.

"Relax, Owl, I'll get us out of here," said Pangera.

"I can't suspect or admit the power of that magnitude," said the admiral.

"We'll just have to give it time," said Pangera. The Starfleet kept on fighting.

Meanwhile, on the planet, the freedom fighters had split up to help the Mingklins fight in different areas along with Heavenly Federal soldiers. Tiblo and Manda fought off some troopers guarding the bunker.

"We'll need some reinforcements," said Tiblo.

Manda contacted the other freedom fighters, "Shana, Skinamar! Where are you?!"

"We're right here!" said Shana through her communicator.

"We need you guys at the bunker right away!" said Manda.

"We're on our way!" said Shana as she turned off her communicator. "Come on, Skinamar."

Skinamar followed Shana back to the bunker. Trouble was happening both on the planet and in outer space.

Chapter 25

Boomer and Waternoose Face Off

Meanwhile, in the Palace of Sharp, the emperor said, "Your fleet has lost . . . and your friends on the planet surface will not survive. Now take your weapon and strike me down. I am out of my immortality."

Nala Boomer realized she had no choice. She used the force of her mind to grab her zorcher from the emperor. Darth Waternoose activated his light saber. Nala tried to zap the emperor, but Waternoose blocked the shot with his saber. The emperor laughed. And so, Nala and Waternoose finally began to fight. Nala fired her zorcher repeatedly while Waternoose wielded his light saber. They fought around the emperor's throne. At the edge where the stairs led down, Nala made a surprise kick at Waternoose's belly. Waternoose fell backward. The emperor laughed. Waternoose flipped as he hovered over the stairs until he fell to the lower floor, landing on his rear.

"Good," said the emperor. "Very good indeed."

Waternoose stood up on his crab legs and said, "Artidector has taught you well."

Nala leaped up to a nearby pipe intersection just like a real lioness, then swung on a bar, and flipping up on a metal rack balcony.

"Your thoughts betray you, Waternoose," she said. "Your family is in heaven; and I was there, too. Think of the conflict."

"There is no conflict," said Waternoose as he approached near the balcony.

"I will not fight you, Bonula," said Nala.

"You cannot deny what you must do," said Waternoose. "A battle is what counts for both of us. If you will not fight . . . you will meet your destiny." He threw his light saber up to the balcony and Nala jumped down. The saber sliced bars and racks. Nala was trapped in a junk heap. She hid under it as Waternoose opened his belly cabinet to swing all of his robotic tentacles snapping their claws trying to grab Nala out of hiding. Nala shot her zorcher at them repeatedly. One of the tentacles smoked and fell apart.

Chapter 26

The Battle for Sorina

War continued in the jungles of Sorina. As Serpential walkers terrorized the forest, a surprising strategy was made. Thumps got on one walker. A Mingklin peered into the view window and taunted the driver.

"Hey!" said the driver. Two Mingklins with Regulto Beauxon and Steve Irwin were on top of the walker. Regulto opened the top hatch. The two Mingklins jumped inside. Regulto lifted the driver out.

"What is the meaning of this?" the driver asked. Regulto threw him off the walker. He and Steve fell inside. Regulto took over the controls.

"I knew you had it in you, Regulto," said a reflection of Rufus the beast in the view window. Regulto winked his eye. He began to drive the walker around. He found another walker and shot it with the blasters of the walker he stole.

Meanwhile, a bunch of Mingklins carried a vine net of coconuts. They cut it open when an enemy walker passed by. The coconuts spilled and rolled down the hill. The walker walked by and stepped on them, slipping and tripping after breaking some of them. The walker fell on the ground and exploded.

In a high tree, a Mingklin swung on a vine tied to a log while another Mingklin did the same thing in another tree. They both collided into a walker and blew it up.

A walker shot at some Mingklins with explosions on the ground. The Mingklins ran off and hid behind trees. One Mingklin was burned and wounded and can no longer move. Guk went to him and tried to talk to him, but the burned Mingklin died.

And so, five of the freedom fighters along with a band of Heavenly Federal soldiers fought off scale troopers with blasters. Shana and Skinamar tried to crack the code again to enter the bunker. Manda fended off enemy blaster shots with her light saber. One shot burned her shoulder. She fell to the bunker's outer wall.

"Manda!" shouted Tiblo. He dashed to her and everyone ceased fire. Troopers approached them. Tiblo looked at Manda in the eyes and said, "You were like a daughter to me."

"I know," said Manda.

"Alright, freeze!" said a trooper.

"We're freezing," said Skinamar.

Shana threw her boomerang at the troopers, knocking them out one by one. It came back to her. Meanwhile, draco troopers found treason made by one walker driver. The walker driven by Regulto shot them down. It surprised the Heavenly Federal soldiers and freedom fighters as it shot more troopers out of the way. All of the Serpential troopers retreated and the freedom fighters put their hands or paws up. The walker approached them. The hatch opened and out came Regulto and Steve.

"Oy there!" said Steve.

"Captain!" said Regulto.

"Reg, Steve!" said Tiblo. "Get down here, Manda's wounded!"

"We're coming!" said Regulto.

"No, wait!" Tiblo shouted.

"What?!"

"Uh . . . stay right there!" Tiblo turned to Manda and said, "I got an idea."

Manda stood up and said, "What now?"

"Everyone move aside!" Tiblo commanded the others to get clear of the entrance. He turned to the walker and shouted, "Fire!"

Regulto got back to the controls an activated the blasters and shot at the bunker's doors. The entrance exploded. Tiblo ran to the soldiers.

"Do you have the charges?" he asked.

"Yep," said a bear soldier. "Packages of them."

"Bring 'em," said Tiblo. The soldiers followed him carrying the packages of explosive charges.

Back in outer space, Heavenly Federal pilots barely had a chance to survive the battle with the flying pirate knights. Pangera contacted the admiral and said, "Well,

Admiral, we're about to stand a few chances against that biosphere."

"All power to command!" the admiral ordered the pilots. "Fire at all targets in your path. The soldiers should be in the bunker by now." Everyone followed orders.

CHAPTER 27

THE SERPENTIAL CONSEQUENCE

Nala Boomer hid from Darth Waternoose within a dark place of the palace as Waternoose looked everywhere for her.

"You cannot hide forever, Nala," he said.

"I will not fight you!" Nala exclaimed. Waternoose finally found her under a ramp next to a table of computers.

"You cannot deny your destiny," said Waternoose, "neither can you deny your fate. You must face what you are called for. It is the only way you can save your friends." He had many different thoughts seeking time with his top three eyes. "Your thoughts betray you as well." Then he sought the future about the freedom fighters. "A prince and a princess. Your federation has a brother prince and a sister princess. Your feelings have now betrayed them, too. It will be a matter of time until that princess is brought back to life and reunited with her brother. If you will not repent to the Serpent's Ghost . . . then perhaps *they* will." He set his light saber in front of him using both hands.

Nala jumped out of hiding and fired her zorcher, shouting, "NEVER!" The fighting continued. Waternoose wielded his light saber and knocked one of the computers off the table nearby. The two fighters moved across the second deck, then down the stairs to the lowest deck near the elevator. Waternoose was about to face his last stand against Nala. She zapped his light saber away and then zapped his right hand. The hand fell apart. It showed inner circuits sparking, Waternoose fell to the floor, admitting defeat.

Suddenly, the emperor walked down the stairs, laughing and cackling until he said, "Good! Your revenge is complete. Now you are honored to be my new servant with the Serpent's Ghost haunting you."

Nala turned off her zorcher. "Never," she said. She threw her zorcher across the deck and said, "I'll never repent to the Serpent's Ghost." She caught her breath and breathed moderately. "You've failed, your highness. I am a freedom fighter . . . like I was in my previous life."

The emperor looked at her and hissed, saying, "So be it, freedom fighter."

CHAPTER 28

THE SHIELD IS DOWN

Meanwhile, Tiblo Tigro helped some Heavenly Federal soldiers plant explosive charges inside the bunker. They were all set for one minute.

"Well, that's the last of them," said Tiblo as they finished setting the charges. "Let's go!" They all ran out. "Everybody, take cover!" All the soldiers and freedom fighters ran into the jungle awaiting the explosion of the charges. The minute passed and the bunker was finally destroyed. A huge explosion blasted pieces of it away.

In outer space, the admiral announced, "The shield is down!" He commanded some pilots to head for the Death Scale. The instructions were to enter a crevice within the volcanic area.

"I'm going in!" said Pangera.

"Oo-hoo-hoo!" cried the owl. Pangera flew the Great Red Shark toward the Death Scale heading for the volcanoes.

CHAPTER 29

THE END OF THE EMPEROR

Inside the palace, Emperor Sharp approached Nala Boomer with a more fearsome consequence.

"If you will not repent," he said, "you will be destroyed." He put up his hands and secreted lightning from his fingertips at Nala. She fell forward on the floor and suffered the electrocution. The emperor laughed and stopped the lightning.

"Nothing can save you now," he said. "Only now and then do you understand." He secreted his lightning again. As this happened, Waternoose awoke from his defeated place and then stood up on his legs and approached where the emperor tortured Nala. Once again the lightning stopped.

"You are weak," said the emperor. "Now everything comes to your lack of courage." He secreted a third amount of lighting. Waternoose watched the tragedy go on. The emperor hissed in fury.

"Keanu," said Nala as she was covered in lightning, "please . . . help!" The lightning stopped.

"And now," said the emperor, "Nala Boomer . . . you will die . . . again."

Nala tried to get up off the floor, but the emperor secreted more lightning and this time, he decided not to stop until Nala was dead again. Waternoose felt inside himself a real heart of a former hero which he once was before his first death. He had thoughts of it in his head as he watched the emperor try to spit venom at Nala. Suddenly, Waternoose went to the emperor and grabbed him, lifting him up with his mechanical tentacles.

"Ah," said the emperor, "what are you doing?"

"You cannot destroy what was once destroyed before," said Waternoose. The emperor tried to electrocute him from above. Waternoose approached the elevator shaft.

"We were supposed to have the most powerful empire in the galaxy until it's over," said the emperor.

"No," said Waternoose. "It *is* over." He threw the emperor down the elevator shaft. The emperor screamed as he fell, still secreting lightning. Waternoose watched his former master fall to his doom. He fell into the lava at the bottom of Serpentopolis. Then suddenly a swarm of whitish teal clouds filled the shaft with lightning raging everywhere. Then an image of the emperor's skeleton appeared. And so, Emperor Hieronymus Sharp was defeated. Waternoose breathed heavily through his mask. He was falling to the floor. Nala grabbed him and started dragging him away from the throne room and down the elevator.

Suddenly, the two vulture viceroy brothers, Hooker and Blunt Volton, flew down and toward a speaker system.

"Treachery!" said Hooker as he activated it. "Our emperor has been destroyed!"

"By Waternoose!" shouted Bunt. Scale troopers and Serpential officers patrolled every hall. Nala knew she had to remain stealthy.

Meanwhile, Pangera Pelwoski led some Heavenly Federal pilots down into the volcanic crevice and into the tunnels that led to the Death Scale's core.

CHAPTER 30

KEANU BONULA

Patrols happened everywhere inside Serpentopolis. Nala Boomer found a good hiding place as scale troopers ran by. Nala looked at Darth Waternoose.

"Boomer," said Waternoose. "Help me take this mask off."

"But you'll die," said Nala.

Waternoose breathed and said, "Nothing can stop that now. For once I must face you with my own eyes. Do it."

Nala carefully detached the top part of Waternoose's mask, then uncovered the face by taking off the front part. The face appeared to be a human with a completely different voice. He breathed rapidly and said, "Nala Boomer . . . you were right about me. Go, my friend . . . leave me."

"No," said Nala. "You're coming with me. I can't leave you here, I've got to save you."

Keanu Bonula said slowly, "You already have. Go . . . tell your friends that . . . you were right. Say the word 'Ohana' and leave."

"Keanu," said Nala. "I won't leave you."

Bonula started dying and he said, "Say 'Ohana' and I will return to heaven."

"Ohana," said Nala. Keanu Bonula finally died. Knowing that the Death Scale was about to be destroyed, Nala ran down to the hangar where she and Waternoose flew into in the shuttle.

CHAPTER 31

THE DEATH SCALE'S DESTRUCTION

Deep in the tunnels under the Death Scale's surface, Pangera led pilots searching for the core. Outside, the admiral commanded, "Concentrate all fire, we merely have a chance to win."

"We're going in," said Pangera. He came to an open place where they all found a large, blue, sparkling ball of energy that held things up with power.

"That's it!" said Pangera. "Ready, aim, fire!" All pilots fired at the Death Scale's core. It began to explode in a matter of minutes. The pilots fled as fast as they could. Meanwhile, Nala Boomer flew a shuttle out of one of Serpentopolis's hangars and away from the Death Scale. Pangera and his fellow pilots flew out of the volcanic crevice. A scale destroyer was blown up and it fell on the Death Scale's surface near its jungle and exploded. Officers activated defense guns from a control tower.

"Activate all firing systems!" said one of them.

"Too late!" shouted another one. All those officers jumped down the tower's shaft as a Heavenly Federal pilot shot the tower. Pilots fled, as a few were fried by the explosion. The Death Scale suddenly blew up into smithereens. Soon it was all space dust. It formed a supernova over Sorina. The Mingklins jumped for joy and victory. All soldiers and freedom fighters watched it as well.

"I sure hope Nala Boomer wasn't on that thing when it blew," said Tiblo.

"She wasn't," said Manda. "I can feel it."

"Me, too," said Martino.

"Do you really care for her?" Tiblo asked.

"Sure," said Martino. "After all, she's my hero."

"I knew you had it in you, Marty," said Skinamar.

Suddenly, a voice called in the freedom fighters' heads. Meanwhile, General Gando Grizzle was hurt. Tiblo went to him.

"Tiblo Tigro," said the general. "My legs hurt from this log."

"General, here," said Tiblo show him his paw.

"Take my badge," said the general. "You're general now. I must wait for a hospital ship. I'm about to retire." He gave his badge to Tiblo. He took it from him. And now he is "General Tiblo Tigro". The voice calling the freedom fighters was Artidector. They followed a path that led them away from the jungle.

"It sounds like Artidector," said Martino. "I wonder where he is."

"That's what we're gonna find out," said Tiblo.

"How can he need our help and what for?" asked Shana. "He's a god."

"Bungle jungles," said Steve Irwin. "Another day of hunting." The whole team followed a path of dirt that allowed them to journey through miles of misty fog untold to be part of the planet.

CHAPTER 32

ARTIDECTOR IN CHAINS

Beyond the mist, the freedom fighters found Artidector in a large frame of energy chains binding his limbs.

"Artidector!!" all the heroes exclaimed.

"Brain Tentacles has imprisoned me," said Artidector. "Beneath here is a power box that keeps him alive. Destroy it!" The freedom fighters tried to snatch the metal power box under the frame, but suddenly, Brain Tentacles' mutant alien minions appeared blocking their way. Brain Tentacles emerged from a puddle of slime. He grabbed his power box and laughed, mocking the freedom fighters, saying, "If it were only that easy, fools, you might destroy *me* as well."

"Freedom fighters!" Artidector called out. "Save yourselves!"

"Not this time," said Martino. "This time we fight."

Brain Tentacles disappeared in the distance as the freedom fighters battle the mixed aliens. Martino used his disk launcher while aliens dodged the flying disks. Squirmwarg lunged his magma worm head at the heroes and Manda sliced the head off with her light saber. The three-eyed green alien, Grick and the fish-finned, one-eyed alien, McGriggle surrounded Tiblo and he burned with fury that overcame the two aliens, knocking them backward. Martino used his imagination, closing his eyes and feathered wings appeared on his outspread arms. The aliens were surprised. Shana leaped up high in the air and threw her boomerang at Vraught, the ant-headed, scorpion-bodied alien.

"They've got powers!" cried Grick.

"Retreat!" shouted McGriggle. All the aliens gave up and fled the fight. Tiblo and Martino shot the energy chains that held Artidector. All the freedom fighters gathered around him. Artidector had a long story to tell them.

"About time I told you the truth," he began, "Nala Boomer once had courage since her mother died. But it was corrupted by the emperor's poisonous nightmare powers."

"At least she's with us, now," said Skinamar.

"Emperor Sharp used a magic curse that made him and his followers immortal," Artidector continued. "You can break this curse by following this stone path . . ." he showed the freedom fighters a path of stones nearby. ". . . there are sacred words that will help defeat the Sharp Empire forever. Now that the emperor is dead, we shall be rid of his soldiers and monsters."

"And there's more," said Martino, "my sister the princess and the Phantom of the Galaxy."

"The princess is placed on a pedestal beyond this place," said Artidector. "My children are ready for me."

"That phantom could be hiding anywhere," said Tiblo.

"We're all doomed!" said Manda.

"Something bad is gonna happen!" said Shana.

"I believe everything you say," said Artidector. "But there is nothing I can do. What we need is an amount of patience. Go and follow your next path. Victory for heroism is waiting for you." The freedom fighters followed the stone path within the mist. There appeared to be a great labyrinth where the Sharp Empire celebrated its immortality.

Chapter 33

The Serpential Legacy

The strange labyrinth had hieroglyphs of Serpential pirate knights invading different worlds.

"Hey, this must be where all the Serpential forces won battles against many civilizations," said Martino.

"That's my family," said Manda as she found one picture.

"My aunt and uncle's farm," said Martino as he found another picture.

"Talk about bringing back memories," said Skinamar.

Suddenly, an illusion of Emperor Sharp appeared. It scared off the freedom fighters. Tiblo and Martino ran in one direction while the others went another way. In each direction was an unexpected staircase which everyone fell and toppled down. Skinamar, Steve, Regulto, Shana, and Manda found themselves near a tower of research with a library and a laboratory above it.

"A library?" said Regulto.

"Where exactly are we?" asked Skinamar.

"Where are Tiblo and Martino?" asked Manda.

"I can't reach them on the communicator," said Shana as she tried to work her wrist communicator. "I hope they're alright."

Tiblo and Martino slid on a slide down and up on a ramp near a tower. They walked up the stairs.

"Where do you think we are?" asked Martino.

"We'll probably find out at the top of this tower," said Tiblo. They climbed up in the tower's house and outside a window, Martino found the ice crystal containing his sister out on top of a pyramid ahead. Tiblo's wrist communicator beeped. He answered it. Holograms of the others appeared.

"Are you guys okay?" asked Shana.

"We're in the middle of a bad situation," said Tiblo.

"We're in some kind of watch tower and I found my sister on a pyramid outside," said Martino.

"Oh boy!" said Skinamar. "The princess is here."

"Crikey!" said Steve. "I hear dinosaurs." A roaring sound came from far away. A band of pirate knights that fled from the exploding Death Scale emerged in the labyrinth.

"We gotta find a way out of here," said Tiblo. "Can you find a way to cover us?"

"Sure," said Shana. "There are laser cannons up in the place we're at."

"We'll find a way out eventually," said Manda.

"Just hang in there, guys," said Skinamar. The communication system was turned off.

Suddenly, a strange, ghostly siren sound came by the watch tower heading for the princess.

"What was that?" asked Tiblo.

"I don't know," said Martino. "But I think we're gonna find out."

At the research tower, the five remaining freedom fighters climbed up a stairway to the top floor where a lab of computers was with multiple remote control laser cannons sat on top. At each of four corners, there were remote control panels that controlled six cannons each. Regulto did research on one of the computers on the table in the middle of the room. Skinamar, Shana, Manda, and Steve activated the control panels. They started to control the laser cannons to fire at the pirate knights, walking on foot and flying in ships.

"This is just like the arcade," said Skinamar. He fired at as many targets as he could along with Steve, Manda, and Shana. Regulto found out about the curse of immortality, which the Sharp Empire lived with. Pirate knight ships fired at the laser cannons, shooting them down one by one.

"Whoa, crikey," said Steve. "I'm losing guns."

"Me, too," said Skinamar.

"Woo-hoo!" Shana shouted with excitement firing down many pirate knight ships.

Steve lost all his laser cannons. "And I'm out," he said. He went by Regulto at the computers. Regulto picked up information of words that created the immortal curse. They said "Lucifer Satan Cobra".

Meanwhile, Tiblo and Martino walked down from the watch tower and found a wall with carvings of Emperor Sharp. They found the three same words on the bottom.

"Lucifer Satan Cobra," Martino read them. "That's Emperor Sharp. He must have used these words to become immortal and create his empire."

Back in the research tower, Skinamar ran out of laser cannons. "Game over for me," he said.

"I have it!" shouted Regulto. He ran to a window and shouted, "LUCIFER SATAN COBRA!" The pirate knights heard it all.

"No!" said one of them. "They found our secret spell. Our immortality is broken." Martino and Tiblo fought off the pirate knights with their weapons. The pirate knights started to fall dead after their curse was broken. Ships and laser cannons fired back and forth on the research tower. Laser guns were being destroyed. Manda ran out of firepower.

"RRGH! I'm out!" she scolded.

Shana was the last one firing the guns. Pirate knights took out most of the remaining guns.

"Fantastic," she said, "I only have two guns left." She fired the last two cannons as the others were out to fight the pirate knights. Regulto took a dose of his medicine, so that Rufus the beast could take over for him. Shana ran out of her cannons.

"Well, guys," she said, "it's been fun."

Everybody went down to the labyrinth's battleground to reunite. Pirate knights were really dying.

"So *that's* it," said Skinamar. "Those three words are mentioned to take away their immortality. We gotta tell the others."

Rufus took on many pirate knights. He threw a crocodile around and that knight landed by a pedestal with a potion.

"Come on!" Rufus growled. "Show me what you've got." The crocodilian pirate knight grabbed the potion.

"No!" Rufus shouted. The knight drank the potion.

"Not the whole thing," said Rufus as his face changed to a worried look. The knight finished off the flask and took off his armor as he started to transform.

All the other pirate knights retreated and ran away. Skinamar approached Martino and Tiblo.

"Hey, guys!" he called out. "We found out what made the Serpentials immortal."

"So did we, Skinamar," said Martino.

Rufus fought against the transformed pirate knight who transformed into a gorilla-muscled crocodile.

"I am Gorocodile!" he growled. As Rufus tried fighting him, Gorocodile knocked him back. This beast was stronger than Rufus.

"Tiblo, Martino!" said Rufus. "Run!"

"I'll handle this," said Tiblo. He put up his blasters and repeatedly fired at Gorocodile. Suddenly, Gorocodile slammed the ground to create a stone crack under Tiblo. The crack widened and Tiblo fled from it.

"He's too strong," he said.

"We're doomed!" said Martino.

"No," said Rufus. "He's burning in fury and pain. He'll soon change back." Gorocodile snuck behind him and put his head in his mouth and hugged him in a wrestler's way.

"Tiblo!" Rufus cried. "Help!" Tiblo took his laser pocket knife and put it in his mouth and ran on all fours and pounced up. He turned his knife on and plunged it into Gorocodile's right arm. He turned his knife off the instant Gorocodile roared in pain. Rufus was free from his grip. Gorocodile held his wounded arm and rested aside.

"My medicine's done," said Rufus.

"Let's go!" shouted Martino. "To the pyramid!" All the freedom fighters headed for the pyramid with the ice crystal that held Princess Mariana Izodorro. They all ran as Gorocodile came up with his healing wound.

"You'll pay for that!" he shouted. He started to run after the freedom fighters. "Give me a real fight!" Suddenly, Steve Irwin grabbed his jaws with his whip and jumped on top of his head.

"Alright, you big lizard!" he said. "Take this!" He held a knife and stabbed the top of his head. Gorocodile roared as the knife got stuck, stabbing his brain. Steve leaped off the beast as it roared, and ran away in pain until he died. Soon the freedom fighters all gathered by the base of the pyramid. There they met Genghis Monka.

"Freedom fighters," he said.

"Father!" said Manda.

"Genghis Monka!" said Tiblo, Martino, and Skinamar.

"I must warn you," Genghis explained, "Brain Tentacles is about to destroy your princess with a detonation device."

"Oh no," said Martino. "That's my sister. We've gotta stop him!"

"Be careful," said Genghis. All the freedom fighters followed the up way of the pyramid to the top. Genghis went to another place on its side.

Chapter 34

The Battle of Brain Tentacles

Just as the freedom fighters reached the top of the pyramid, Brain Tentacles planted the detonator in front of the pedestal with the frozen princess.

"This will be a day long remembered," he said.

"Oh no," said Martino. "We're too late!"

"You've come at the right moment to say good bye to your precious princess, freedom fighters," said Brain Tentacles as he turned to them. "Now, this is where it *really* ends." He lit his light saber.

"Bring it!" said Martino as he put up his disk launcher. Brain Tentacles reached out his tongue plant hand's tongue to grab the disk launcher and he ran off down the pyramid's slope.

"Catch me if you can!" he shouted.

"You guys go after him and I'll take care of the detonator," said Skinamar. He went by the pedestal as the freedom fighters went after Brain Tentacles. Skinamar picked up the detonator and found that it was blinking faster and faster. He quickly ran away from the pedestal and threw the detonator high in the sky. Then it exploded with blue light forming a great drum.

At one side of the pyramid, the freedom fighters began to fight Brain Tentacles. He dropped Martino's disk launcher and Martino grabbed him.

"You may have defeated the Sharp Empire once and for all," said Brain Tentacles. "But it's not over yet—you must face me!" He wielded his light saber. Tiblo set his blasters ready for combat.

"Captain Tigro," said Brain Tentacles.

"It's *General* Tigro now," said Tiblo. They started fighting. Tiblo fired his blasters as Brain Tentacles wielded his saber to deflect the shots. Tiblo made a move by sneaking under Brain Tentacles. He shot his chin and used his laser knife to cut off some of his tentacles.

"Augh!" Brain Tentacles screamed. "You'll pay for that!" He stabbed Tiblo in the back with his steel crustacean claw. Tiblo screamed in pain.

"Tiblo!" shouted Martino.

"One down, six to go," said Brain Tentacles.

Tiblo rested on his front with his paws supporting his weight on the ground. Martino was next to fight Brain Tentacles. Skinamar returned to the others. Tiblo found Brain Tentacles' power box resting ahead of him. Brain Tentacles' sliced-off tentacles came to life and guarded the power box. Genghis Monka appeared with a light saber. He lit it and called his daughter.

"Manda," he said, "I have no choice. Forgive me." It seemed that if his mind were controlled. He wielded his saber as Manda wielded hers.

"Stop!" she said. "I will not fight you, Father!" She ran from him.

As Martino and Brain Tentacles fought, Brain Tentacles unleashed his tongue plant hand's tongue to reach out and choke Martino. He threw him aside.

"Two down, five to go," said Brain Tentacles.

"Marty," said Skinamar as he approached Martino.

Tiblo found a rock that he could use to smash the power box with as he approached it. He fought the undead tentacles away. Manda fought Brain Tentacles in a light saber duel.

"You'll pay for your wrong doings!" said Manda. Brain Tentacles made popping sounds with his mouth as he frowned.

Suddenly, a demonic voice occurred through the air saying, "Brain Tentacles!" The fighting stopped as everyone heard the voice. It continued, "You are no longer a use of me!" The freedom fighters wondered what it was and where it came from.

"Who are you?!" asked Brain Tentacles. "I demand you to show yourself!"

"I am the one whom you brought here," said the voice. "Only the Heaven Federation can see me, but *you* cannot!"

"I . . ." said Brain Tentacles, "I don't understand."

The voice laughed then it said, "I thought you would not. Now give the freedom fighters what they were looking for."

"As you wish," said Brain Tentacles. He grabbed two tubes of a blue potion from his tentacle beard with his crustacean claw and held them out. "Take one of these. They are revival potions. Use one to heal any friends or bring some back to life." Manda took the potion at the front of his claw.

"I didn't think he'd be generous," said Skinamar.

"You think I'm generous, freedom fighters?!" Brain Tentacles roared and gurgled as he charged at the freedom fighters. Tiblo smashed the power box with the rock in his paw. Brain Tentacles started to scream as he felt electricity raging in his body causing him to shrivel and fall apart. Tiblo smashed the box again and again as hard as he could. Brain Tentacles started to leak phlegm and he exploded with green and orange colored vomit-like slime. His skeleton fell out and the father brain that formed his head came to life as it was once again itself. Manda fled the slimy mess.

"Oh gross," said Shana. It was the end of Brain Tentacles.

"Our master is dead," said Grick from nearby the pyramid. Suddenly, he and McGriggle began to change back into humans. The rest of Brain Tentacles' followers changed into simple aliens and they all went their separate ways. Manda approached Tiblo and poured a drop of the revival potion on his back. The stab wounds healed.

"We'll take that other potion," said Grick and McGriggle as they climbed up and took the potion from the puddle of slime.

"There they go," said Martino.

Artidector's voice occurred in all the freedom fighters' heads, "Come! The princess awaits." Six celestial white condors flew to the top of the pyramid.

"Artidector's children," said Martino.

"The princess!" said Tiblo.

"Come on, guys!" said Skinamar. The freedom fighters followed the way up to the top of the pyramid.

CHAPTER 35

THE PRINCESS'S REVIVAL

Up on top, Artidector's children surrounded the ice crystal with the frozen princess. They made a heavenly circle around her. The freedom fighters got up there and Martino ran toward the pedestal.

"What's going on?!" he shouted. "You said this would *save* her!"

"Marty, are you crazy?" asked Tiblo.

One of the condors started to fly straight at the crystal. As he did, he imploded inside and the princess's gag loosened and fell off. The ice melted inside.

"No!" Martino shouted. He ran toward the crystal as the other condors imploded as they warped inside. The princess's binders came off. Soon she was coming back to life on Artidector's behalf. The young condors flew out and zoomed toward their father, floating in midair.

"Wake up!" Martino said to his sister. "Wake up!" The ice crystal began to crack and explode with water splashing. The princess was alive once again. She was all wet. Martino set his eyes on her as he approached her. The princess coughed out the water.

"Mariana," said Martino.

"Martino," said Princess Mariana Izodorro, "brother, is it really you?"

"Yes," said Martino. "We were very young. We went our separate ways. I have friends with me." The princess stood up.

"It's a pleasure to meet you, your highness," said Manda.

"Gosh," said Shana. "I've never met a princess before."

Skinamar skipped up and down shouting, "Hooray! Our princess has returned!"

"But what happened?" asked the princess. "I thought I drowned."

"The Sharp Empire executed you," said Tiblo. "And our holy friend, Artidector, and his children now brought you back to life."

The ghost of Zinger Warsp appeared next to Artidector.

"Don't worry, princess," said Zinger. "Your brother has his good eyes on you."

Regulto bowed before the princess saying, "Your majesty."

"Yes, sir!" exclaimed Martino. "The princess is back safe and sound!"

Suddenly, an object from space entered the foggy sky. It was the cobra head of the Palace of Sharp floating above the labyrinth and over the freedom fighters.

"I am reborn!" it said, having the same voice that spoke to Brain Tentacles. "The mighty Serpential god." The object laughed hard. "Kneel all those who stand before me!" It laughed again.

"We will never kneel to you!" said the princess. She walked to her brother and grabbed his disk launcher. "Give me that!"

"Hey, wait!" said Martino. "Well thanks for nothing, sis. Zinger got me those things from our father."

"One of his disk launchers," said the princess. "Well done, brother." She tried shooting at the cobra head.

"We gotta do something, guys!" said Skinamar.

"Our ships!" Tiblo remembered. Everybody found their ships at the bottom of the pyramid. They ran down there as the princess remained on top, firing the disk launcher. The freedom fighters hopped in their ships and flew up to a vortex in the sky to follow the flying cobra head.

Chapter 36

The Phantom's Revelation

The vortex led to an empty place in space. The freedom fighters flew and followed the giant cobra head. The head turned around and what appeared to be a giant, white, hideous demonic figure with six slit eyes, long needle-like fangs and hands with long pointed fingers.

"I have been looking forward to this day," it said, "to see you in person, freedom fighters!"

"It's the phantom from the gem!" said Martino.

"He is hideous," said Manda.

"He's scaring me to death!" said Shana.

"You're telling me," said Regulto.

"And now," said the phantom, "to destroy the ENTIRE UNIVERSE!" It raised its hands up and turned around.

"We've gotta stop this thing!" shouted Tiblo.

"We're ahead of you, Tiblo," said the others. They all started to attack the cobra head connected to the Phantom of the Galaxy. They all fired their guns at the eyes. The cobra's mouth opened and Tiblo fired a missile into it. It exploded making the cobra head crack. The phantom laughed, "Ho hah HAW!" It turned around and showed its face roaring with its hands spread out.

"Go for its hands!" shouted Tiblo. All the freedom fighters shot their guns at the phantom's hands. The phantom moved one hand at a time to fight the freedom fighters. Each hand cracked like ceramic. It clapped its hands against the heroes as they dodged them and the hands broke. The phantom roared in anger. Suddenly, it began to vacuum the freedom fighters into its mouth. The heroes struggled to escape. Suddenly, a bomb exploded behind the phantom. The cobra head was destroyed. It was Nala Boomer in her fighter ship.

"Hey, guys!" she called to them. "You look like you needed a hand with this monster!"

"Nala!" cried Skinamar as the freedom fighters were saved from being vacuumed.

"I can't believe it!" said Martino.

Then a swarm of fighter ships led by the Great Red Shark arrived to fight the phantom. Ships fired lasers into the phantom's eyes. It was getting angrier and angrier.

"Hey, Tiblo!" said Pangera Pelwoski. "You're stuck with a space ghost and you might need a panther's help. It's good to see you, buddy!"

"We must destroy the Phantom of the Galaxy before it does something bad!" said Tiblo. The phantom's eyes turned red. It started to vacuum ships again.

"Fire missiles in the open mouth!" shouted Tiblo. All pilots followed orders as some of them fired the missiles in the phantom's mouth. It caused its head to open like an envelope.

"Alright!" Tiblo said. "Now go for the brain!" The pilots shot lasers at the phantom's brain. The phantom moved around and swooped at a pilot to make him crash.

"I'm hit!" he shouted. He burned up and flew out of sight. The phantom's head closed and it was cracking like an egg. It opened its mouth roaring out loud. The pilots shot more missiles into its gape. The head opened once again to show its brain. The pilots all shot at it and it burned red.

"Cease fire!" commanded Tiblo. The phantom's head closed. Its cracks all turned red and yellow and it began to scream out loud. It screamed so loud that it filled many ears on planets near and far. Everybody flew away from the awful sight. The phantom began to explode into a blue and white supernova. And so, the entire war of the Sharp Empire and the Heaven Federation was over.

CHAPTER 37

THE END OF THE WAR

All pilots and the freedom fighters flew back down to Sorina. Princess Mariana Izodorro was with the Mingklins. The Mingklins played instruments made out of wood, coconuts, and scrap metal. One Mingklin used trooper helmets for a drum set. The Mingklins sang a party song of victory for the Heaven Federation. Artidector appeared there along with the ghosts of Zinger Warsp and Keanu Bonula. Nala Boomer met them all face to face. Martino did as well. He went to his sister.

"Thank you, Martino," said the princess.

"Call me, Marty," said Martino.

Regulto showed up and said, "I've decided to marry her."

"She's all yours, Reg," said Martino.

Rufus the beast showed his face in a nearby piece of metal and spoke to Regulto, "I am proud of you, Regulto.

Now I shall leave you." He disappeared and Regulto could see a reflection of himself. He was satisfied and felt happy.

"I've never felt so happy," he said as he shed tears. He had a bell in his pack that he received from Zinger years before. Martino played his lyre, another instrument from Zinger. Manda played her harp and Shana played her flute.

"It's time for a song that I am about to sing!" the princess announced. She raised her arms to lead the music as everyone began playing the right tune for her song. She started singing:

"I was trapped in ice for so many years
An evil has spread out so many fears
Somebody came and took me back
To a place somewhere, nothing can hold me back
(Chorus)
I finally have a hero to save me from death
That hero has caught my every breath
I finally have a hero to take me back home
With my faith and strength, I'm not alone

The evil has left the galaxy
There is nothing left for you and me
Brother prince and sister princess
Together can make it out of this mess
(Repeat Chorus)

As they listened to the song, the freedom fighters had a mighty strong feeling.

"Mmm," said Tiblo.

"Wonderful singing," said Pangera.

Martino was wandering around having thoughts.

"Beautiful," said Skinamar.

CHAPTER 38

MARTINO GOES HOME

Soon the victory party was over. Martino had made a decision. His friends and his sister followed him walking out by the ships.

"Marty," said Skinamar. "Where are you going?"

"I've decided to leave," said Martino.

"Leave??" asked Skinamar. "It was fun having you with us."

"Wouldn't it be better if you stayed with us?" asked Shana.

"Thanks for everything, guys," said Martino. "Regulto, take care of my sister."

"I will do my best," said Regulto.

Martino opened the Clover Bird's cockpit cover. Manda approached him and asked, "Will you ever back?"

"I guarantee it," said Martino. "You can tell Tiblo he can give me call. We'll keep in touch." He hopped in the Clover Bird and began to take off. Everyone waved good bye to him as he flew up to the sky and into space. He decided to head back to Earth. He set the coordinates and activated the hyper-drive and zoomed out of sight. Martino's memories swam around in his mind. Now it's time for a song:

"Martino is going home back where he belongs
Will his friends ever see him again?
The heroes have righted every wrong
Never fighting like they did back then
All the places are getting old
Now Martino is alone
And he's going home."

After days of light speed, Martino finally reached Earth. He flew into its atmosphere, heading for his home in Ireland.

CHAPTER 39

THE EARTH IS AN IMPOSTOR

As Martino landed in his home place where his aunt and uncle's farm used to be, he did not recognize the place. The sky was all grey with clouds of rain. He walked around for minutes and found a portal that led him to Washington, D.C. He found the Lincoln Memorial, which was changed to "Sharp Memorial". Inside Martino found a stone statue of Emperor Sharp sitting on his throne. A message nearby said:

"For the memory of all evil, Emperor Hieronymus
Sharp was overthrown by a former hero. He is
now enshrined in this labyrinth forever."

Suddenly, flying patrol cars came out of nowhere and in front of the memorial. The police officers were all Serpential descendants. A cassowary grabbed his megaphone and called, "Come out with your hands up!"

Martino put his hands up as he heard the call. He walked out of the memorial to show himself.

"Come forth!" said the cassowary officer. Martino came to the patrol car. The officer locked him in cuffs and said, "You're under arrest for trespassing on government property." He took him in his car and the patrol flew to a prison a few miles away.

As Martino was being taking away, he ruefully said to himself, "What am I doing? I came back to Earth and I'm being arrested. There are Serpentials everywhere. This whole planet is an impostor."

And so, he was placed in prison to do time in a cell. Martino said, "What have I done? I should have stayed with my friends."

Suddenly, one of Artidector's children appeared in Martino's cell. He set out his taloned hand and Martino touched it. The condor flew with him into a white portal that led across the galaxy out of the prison and off of Earth. They traveled through a vortex of white, orange, and pink clouds.

It looks like heaven, Martino thought.

Chapter 40

Artidector's Heaven

Martino and the condor ended up in a place of clouds. Martino was asleep and out of breath while he was carried all the way there. He finally woke up and caught a breath. He found Artidector and his children in heaven.

"Hello, Martino," said Artidector. Martino stood up and looked around him.

"Hey," he said. "How are you guys doing?"

"You are safe from temptation which is why you have been brought here into my heaven," said Artidector.

"Earth has been overrun by Serpentials," said Martino. "But why?" Artidector's children were mute, so they formed a rectangle of clouds and showed a video of things that happened around Earth. Many people screamed in a series of earthly disasters such as tornadoes, earthquakes, tidal waves, and hurricanes. Scale troopers showed themselves firing at signs of children's television and franchise places. It showed the Sharp Empire conquering the whole planet. Then it showed Emperor Sharp and his intelligent evolution as he became emperor creating his followers with magical dark forces. The video was over.

After that ghosts appeared. There was King Archibald Izodorro, Martino's father, and his queen, Morgana.

"Mother? Father?" Martino said in surprise. Then ghosts of his aunt and uncle appeared.

"Uncle Rowan?" Martino said. "Aunt Mara?"

"Now you know the reason why you have come," said Artidector.

And with that, he and Martino along with the young celestial condors disappeared and went to a place never seen before.

CHAPTER 41

A WHOLE NEW WORLD

Back with the Heaven Federation, former general Gando Grizzle contacted the freedom fighters. Tiblo's communicator beeped and he answered it.

"General Tigro!" Grizzle called through as his hologram appeared. "Report your status."

"We lost about ten pilots," said Tiblo, "including Martino Izodorro. He decided to leave us."

The freedom fighters and Heavenly Federal pilots and soldiers were back in space on ships along with the Great Red Shark. They all flew in a hangar part of a newly built space station that was built by workers and robots. Suddenly, as they all walked off board, the freedom fighters' communicators beeped. It was a recorded message of Martino's voice saying, "Guys, it's Marty. I'm coming back . . ."

"Hey! It's Marty!" Shana shouted in excitement.

"Marty?" said Admiral Wolfgang as he walked toward the whole band of heroes. "Marty *who?!*"

"It's Mr. Izodorro talking, sir," said Tiblo. "He's coming back."

The message continued, "I'm with Artidector and his children in heaven. They are building us a new world. Everybody stay calm, you're all gonna love this."

A supernova of heavenly clouds appeared creating a nebula of a new star and a system of planets. Artidector had created a planet much like Earth but with many different landmarks around on it. The entire Heaven Federation headed for that planet in the space station moving all the way there. Soon the station was in its atmosphere. Everybody flew ships down on the planet surface.

"This planet has a gospel forgotten by many creatures on Earth," Artidector announced. "Now that gospel returns to all of us, and on this planet, you shall all live happily ever after—of course, that is in fairy tales." Martino appeared rushing toward his friends.

"Marty!" shouted Tiblo. Martino approached him and shook his paw as Tiblo put one arm around him.

"I'm back," said Martino.

"Nice place we got here," said Tiblo.

"From attacks of the Sharp Empire," said Martino, "fantasies are destroyed."

"And yet," said Tiblo, "fantasies will change."

All the freedom fighters discovered the entire place filled with flower fields, mountains of snow, and a great, shiny lake. They went to that lake and walked to its shore.

They saw reflections of themselves as young animals in the water. Martino looked at himself as a kid and waved to that reflection. He had a memory of himself walking in his uncle's garden gathering vegetables, which it showed in the water.

"Is this the fountain of youth?" he asked.

"It looks like a *lake* of youth," said Skinamar.

Manda looked at her young reflection and waved to it.

"Did you have a great adventure?" the reflection asked with a child-like voice. Manda nodded her head. Suddenly, a ghost appeared near her. She saw it float by. It was her father looking like his plain self without the alien mixture of body parts. He was dead once again. Manda kissed her paw and blew it to her father's ghost.

Later, Regulto danced with Princess Mariana Izodorro, engaged to marry her.

"I don't know if I can sing a song for you, princess," said Regulto.

"Music is always in our minds," said the princess.

"I don't know what to sing," said Regulto.

"Don't worry, Reg," said Skinamar as he appeared nearby. "I got the perfect song." He started the music by leading it with his arms waving in different places every second as creatures of the new planet played the music with the freedom fighters' instruments.

"Talk about a one hit wonder," said Tiblo.

Skinamar started singing:

"It's a whole new world
It's a lot like home where we used to belong

Here is our new home
And nothing can go wrong."

The princess continued the next part of the song:

"A new man in my life
Has given me a never before known right
The evil is vanquished
And there is no further fight."

She and Regulto separated from dancing. Regulto and Skinamar sang together:

"We're in a whole new world . . ."

The princess sang:

"We have the fountain of youth
Happiness is suddenly unfurled
It's hard to believe
That it's a whole new world"

Regulto began to sing as the freedom fighters came by:

"It's a whole new world."

Regulto and the princess:

"It's where we belong together"

Regulto:

"This will be our new home forever"

A musical break happened for the song. Then everybody began to sing together:

"It's a whole new world
It's where we belong together
Our lives are in our own debt
This will be . . . our new home . . . forever"
(Slows down until fades)

The song ended. Meanwhile in outer space an image of Emperor Sharp was there in an empty place with his eyes open. Although he was already defeated, he is now only a memory to our heroes.

THE END

EPILOGUE

A FUTURE FOR THE FREEDOM FIGHTERS

Now that the Sharp Empire has been defeated, the freedom fighters are sure to have descendants. Tiblo has married a tigress and now has a son. Regulto and the princess are blessed with a son of theirs. Shana married a kangaroo on the newly made planet and has two joeys, a son and a daughter. Manda married a wolf pilot and now they have a daughter with Manda's skills. Skinamar has been singing the song with his name and created a son he named, Skinamo-Rooney.

Will there be another evil conquering the galaxy? It is now up to these new descendants to find out.

Original Songs by Tyler Johns:

"Swamp Thug Rap" found in Chapter 2
"I Finally Have a Hero" found in Chapter 37
"Martino Is Going Home" found in Chapter 38
"It's a Whole New World" found in Chapter 41

Other books by Tyler Johns:

The Sharp Empire
The Sharp Empire II: The Serpent Strikes Back
The Sharp Empire III: The Phantom of the Galaxy